AF433494

PRAISE FOR WINDCHASER

— ★ ★ ★ —

"Attention grabbing and flows fluidly. Very easy to read and understand. The story has a good flow of gradually beginning to build up to the sparks for the main plot. Introductions of new characters isn't choppy and flows fluidly, there's mystery and questions left unanswered leaving the reader wanting to keep reading to try and figure out the unspoken mysteries within the pages. There's so much intrigue and instances of leaving you on the edge of your seat. I absolutely loved it."

— *Cambrie Fraiser*, author of the upcoming graphic novel *Geyser Falls*.

"While Windchaser gets off to a bit of a slow start, Achak does a wonderful job of introducing the spirituality and deeply introspective nature of Kieran in those beginning chapters, and by the end of the first conversation between Tessa and Kieran I was hooked. I desperately wanted to see where the bond between the two adventurers would go, and the dynamic personality of Tessa in particular of a strong outer shell with the core of a little girl that just wants to be strong tugs at heartstrings and is a refreshing break from copy-pasted "strong female characters" of many books of this day and age. Windchaser is a strong start for an up-and-coming author and I look forward to seeing more of both Kieran and Tessa, and Achak herself, as their story goes on."

— *Sean Snipes*, author of the upcoming novels *Losing Teeth* and *Draco Beastium Sum*.

WINDCHASER

Book #1 — Light And Shadow

By Achak Mahihkan

Cover By Achak Mahihkan
Interior Design By Achak Mahihkan
Written By Achak Mahihkan
Edited By Achak Mahihkan

Published By Lulu

Twitter/X: @sweetwatergoods
Instagram: sweetwater_goodies
Website: achakmbooks.weebly.com

Title Font: Stars by House Of Lime (1001Fonts)
Font: EB Garamond

Contact The Author: achakm2021@gmail.com

For Sean.
Thank you for inspiring me
to write novels again.

OTHER BOOKS AND SERIES BY ACHAK

★

OUT NOW

Connected Skies Series

The Druid And The Wolf

What You Don't Know About God That Will

Blow Your Mind

A Way Through The Valley

COMING SOON

Finbar —A New Hampshire Wolf-Dog Isekai

Sögu Racer

ACKNOWLEDGMENTS

First off, thank you to my husband for sticking with me through this project; you were the first to read it and tell me it was good. I want to thank Sean Snipes for inspiring me to start this novel, as well as for his participation in proof-reading and reviewing. Two others who have done me a great service in proof-reading and reviewing are Cambrie Fraiser and Rex Nigel.

Thank you to my mother for believing in me and my skills.

Thank you, most of all, to Jesus for bringing me out of my depression and giving me the power to create again.

PROLOGUE

★

'Made it through another day in the flatlands. Tracked and found a thief, with repeat offenses, this evening. Brought him to the chief officer, warm. Got paid 20 gold. Bought food and whiskey. A successful mission.'

Kieran carefully wrote in his journal, accompanied by a roaring fire, a dark bottle of whiskey by his side, and the sounds of nature that permeated the night. A cool breeze swept across the open terrain of the Highland Plains, and flowed through his minty blue fur; the fox grabbed a blanket he had lying around his campsite, and wrapped himself in it.

'*It's gonna get cold tonight,*' he judged.

Once done with his journal entry for the day, he placed his book down by his sleeping spot. He took his drink in his white hand and sipped for a while. The taste of the whiskey was strong and smoky, but that's just how he liked it. It was the perfect way for a hardened, lone bounty hunter to end his day; Kieran loved warmth and things that reminded him of good times. Whiskey was one of those things, and whenever he had the pleasure of enjoying it he always thought of the comradery he'd shared with temporary alliances in his past endeavors. When pairing it with a calm night under a starry sky it was sensational.

He was a loner, so did not have much in the way of friends. He did not stick around long enough to get that far with anyone, but he liked it that way. Besides, most folk just talked way too much, and that wasn't his cup of tea, as they say.

Soon Kieran's eyes became heavy. It had been a lot of work to catch that outlaw; he'd been a smart one, and the hunter could give him that. With the moon growing ever older, the fox made his way crawling on the grass into his tent. It wasn't anything special, but it would shelter him from wind and rain, and that's all that mattered to him.

'Heh. Nothing fancy needed. This is good enough for me,' thought Kieran as he snuggled up in his blanket, smiling with his eyes closed. He nuzzled his pillow and savored the full-body heat

he felt both from the campfire still blazing and from the alcohol. He grabbed his sharp dagger and kept it close to him.

It was absolutely a night of comfort for him, and he loved every bit of it. Yawning, he began to let sleep take him.

As sleep enveloped Kieran Dravenholm, his mind drifted into a realm of dreams and distant memories. Visions of his past adventures danced before his closed eyes, accompanied by the faint crackling of the dying campfire.

In his dreams, he relived the moments of triumph and danger that had shaped him into the skilled bounty hunter he was today. He saw himself traversing treacherous terrains, engaging in exhilarating chases, and facing off against formidable adversaries. Each encounter had been a test of his abilities, both physical and mental, pushing him to his limits and honing his skills with every passing day.

But amidst the memories of battles and victories, there were also fleeting glimpses of his old connections. The occasional nod of gratitude from a grateful villager whose town he had saved, or a shared meal with fellow travelers who had crossed paths with him during his journeys. Though these encounters were short-lived and rare, they held a special place in his heart, reminding him that even in his solitary path, he had made a difference in the lives of others.

As the night grew deeper, Kieran's dreams shifted towards a more tranquil landscape. He found himself walking through a serene forest bathed in moonlight, the gentle rustle of leaves accompanying his steps. The air was crisp, and a sense of peace settled within him. In this ethereal realm, he experienced a fleeting moment of contentment, free from the burdens of his bounty-hunting existence.

In the embrace of sleep, Kieran's mind briefly wandered to thoughts of what lay ahead. The challenges that awaited him, the targets he would pursue, and the unknown paths he would tread. But for now, he allowed himself to revel in the tranquility of the moment, finding solace in the simplicity of his campsite and the soothing whispers of the night.

And so, with a smile lingering on his lips, Kieran surrendered to the embrace of slumber. In the quiet darkness, he drifted into a world where his dreams intermingled with the reality of his journey, fueling his resolve, and fortifying his spirit for the trials that awaited him in the world of Arthos.

CHAPTER ONE

WAYFARER

—★—

As the first rays of dawn filtered through the canvas of Kieran's tent, a soft glow of golden light bathed the interior, gently nudging him awake. He stirred, stretching his limbs, the fatigue of the previous day dissipating as he embraced the promise of a new morning.

It was quite a beautiful thing, something that never got old. Each day was a new chapter, it was surely more than welcome any time.

With practiced grace, the minty blue fox rose from his makeshift bed, feeling the coolness of the earth beneath his paws.

He reached for a small leather pouch resting on a nearby stump, its contents holding a collection of fragrant herbs and dried flowers—a testament to his connection with the natural world. He held it dear, since childhood.

Carefully, he selected a sprig of rich purple-bluish lavender, its soothing aroma filling the air as he tucked it behind his ear, a symbol of calmness and balance.

The dawn was a special time for him; before the trials and dangers that surely lay ahead, Kieran liked to ground himself with calming, happy practices.

He got up and walked a little ways away from his campsite; a few steps brought him to a nearby basin filled with fresh water he had collected the previous evening. He cupped his hands, allowing the cool liquid to cleanse his face, invigorating his senses and awakening his mind.

Drops of water glistened in his blue and golden-white pelt, a refreshing reminder of the world's simple pleasures.

The sun's early shafts of light soon soaked deep into his fur, down to his skin, and warmed him. Leaving the tent behind, Kieran stepped out into the embrace of nature, the cool morning breeze tousling his fur and carrying with it the scent of dew-kissed grass and blooming wildflowers.

With each inhale, he felt a deep connection to the world around him, attuned to its rhythms and whispers.

Perhaps it was not a spiritual experience like he once knew when he was a young kit with his family, but it was a deep connection nonetheless.

After having experienced all he had, his faith had dwindled to not much more than the dying embers of his nightly fire. Kieran valued things all the same; this was the world he lived in, after all; he was a part of it, and it was a part of him. Why shouldn't he love it? It was all he knew, and all he ever would know as far as he was aware.

His gaze shifted towards a nearby cottonwood tree, its sturdy branches offering a natural perch.

With the grace of a predator, Kieran ascended the tree, finding solace in its embrace. From this elevated vantage point, he surveyed the vast expanse before him—the sprawling landscape of Arthos, a tapestry of untamed beauty and undiscovered secrets.

Nothing compared to this land he called his own; to the intrepid fox, the realm was endless as well as ageless. Though it was filled to the brim and running over with political unrest and morally degenerate scumbags here and there. On the other hand, it had its unmatched charm.

It was here, amidst the rustling leaves and the harmonious symphony of joyful bird songs, that Kieran found solace.

He closed his eyes, centering himself in the present moment, a moment free from the burdens of his past and the uncertainties of the future. In this stillness, he cultivated a sense of inner peace, a quiet strength that fortified his spirit.

As the sun ascended higher in the sky, its warm embrace kissing the land, Kieran descended from his perch, returning to his campsite. He kindled a small fire, coaxing it to life with practiced precision.

The crackling flames danced before him, casting a gentle warmth upon his face—a symbol of his resilience in the face of adversity.

From his pack, he retrieved a small bundle of dried herbs—a blend he had crafted himself, designed to invigorate and rejuvenate. With deliberate intent, he sprinkled the mixture onto the flames, releasing an aromatic haze that enveloped him.

Inhaling deeply, he allowed the fragrant smoke to cleanse not only his surroundings but also his mind and soul, purging any lingering doubts or negativity.

With the fire crackling in the background, Kieran settled onto a weathered log, his journal and quill in hand. Each stroke of the quill upon the pages was deliberate, capturing the essence of his experiences, thoughts, and reflections.

Artful images flowed effortlessly, as if guided by an unseen force, each entry a testament to his growth, resilience, and unwavering determination. The final product was a lovely sketch of the landscape as his yellow eyes saw it before him.

Completing his journal entry, Kieran closed the weathered book, its pages filled with tales of triumphs and tribulations, a tangible record of his journey through the world of Arthos.

He glanced at the small silver necklace adorning his neck—its pendant a small blue fluorite crystal shard, a symbol of his commitment to his purpose, a reminder of the lives he had touched and the justice he had served.

With a sense of purpose and renewed vigor, Kieran rose from the log, his morning routine complete. He extinguished the fire and packed up his tent and other belongings into a big backpack. He didn't want to leave a trace of his presence on this beautiful landscape, not even forgetting to take his whiskey bottle.

There was some left, and once it was finished it'd be very useful to hold some other liquid. Everything fitted compactly in his bag, and once he was sure he'd gotten everything, the lonesome fox flung the backpack over his shoulders. He secured his trusty weapons and essential supplies to his belt, making sure everything was in order for the journey ahead.

Taking one last look at the campsite, he reflects on the serenity of the Highland Plains, grateful for the moments of peace it has offered him.

With a confident stride, Kieran sets off, his paw steps marking a path through the tall grasses. Among the morning mist and vast stretch of plains, dew laden flowers speckled the landscape. The vibrant petals appearing soft as silk, the early morning sun dancing across the water droplets in a dazzling array of color. They had all sorts of colors, pleasing to the eye, and Kieran walked among them.

The muscles in the bounty hunter's legs rejoiced at the exercise; his body was most satisfied when on the move. The start of a new journey each day was a profound sensation, and his heart sprung forth across the way. His soul danced and ran full speed ahead to wherever his feet would take him, to wherever he'd end up next.

These were the kinds of moments that summarized his very life; sturdy, free, and peaceful.

On the note of missions, he needed to find another job to complete, and hopefully, the next town he stumbled upon would have some to choose from.

The thrill of adventure coursed through his veins, urging him to seek out new challenges and opportunities. With each step, he scanned the horizon, searching for any sign of civilization.

The vast open flatlands stretched out before him, seemingly endless, but he knew that beyond the undulating landscape, settlements were waiting to be discovered.

Days turned into weeks as Kieran traversed the rugged terrain, occasionally encountering fellow travelers who shared tales of distant lands and untold treasures. He listened intently, gathering information about towns and cities rumored to be teeming with opportunities for brave souls like himself.

Finally, on the horizon, he spotted the telltale signs of human habitation. A cluster of rooftops peaked above the stone walls, lit by a lavender-colored sunset, promising the possibility of rest, resupply, and perhaps most importantly, new missions to embark upon.

As he neared the town, the sound of bustling activity grew louder. The air was filled with the aroma of hearty meals cooking and the distant chatter of voices.

Kieran's heart quickened with anticipation as he approached the town's entrance, his keen eyes scanning the surroundings for the familiar sight of a public bulletin board.

Upon entering the town, Kieran found himself amidst a lively marketplace. Traders hawked their wares, children ran through the streets with gleeful abandon, and the scent of freshly baked bread wafted through the air. It was a vibrant tapestry of life, a place where opportunities and challenges awaited.

His eyes fell upon a wooden board adorned with parchment notices, pinned in an organized fashion. Eagerly, he stepped closer, perusing the various job postings that ranged from escort missions to retrieving rare artifacts and solving local mysteries.

He narrowed his eyes to read and rubbed his white chin naturally, as he often did when in serious work mode. Each notice held the promise of excitement, danger, and the chance to make a difference in the lives of the townsfolk. Plus, of course, food money; that was important!

Kieran's mind thought hard as he considered his options. He weighed the risks and rewards, assessing his skills and strengths. He knew that whichever mission he chose would test his mettle, but that was precisely what he desired.

With a determined glint in his yellow eyes, he plucked a notice from the board—a call for a skilled man to track down a particularly troublesome character known as The Shadow.

The artist of the poster had sketched a black male swift fox with yellow eyes. He seemed to be missing both ears, and his face was covered in deep scars.

'This guy hasn't had a good time, has he?' Kieran huffed sarcastically, with amusement.

The minty fox began to read the included information about The Shadow, and it was made abundantly clear by the excerpt that he was a cunning and relentless criminal, known for his involvement in a variety of nefarious activities.

He excelled in the art of stealth and was known to use his knowledge of the city's intricate alleyways and hidden passages to his advantage. He was a master thief, targeting valuable treasures, artifacts, and even sensitive information.

The Shadow's crimes often involved sophisticated heists, leaving authorities baffled and ordinary citizens living in constant fear.

"Oy!"

Kieran looked around to see a city guard approaching him.

"You clearly fancy yourself a challenge," the guard said, a brown and gold male fox. "We appreciate the zeal, but I want to warn you to be careful."

Kieran brushed off the warning politely, showing his confidence. "I've seen his type a hundred times before," he said.

The brown-and-white fox paused for a moment, unsure what to say, and clearly taken aback by the bounty hunter's manner. "Well, thank you for taking the job we posted," the guard said politely, patting Kieran on the shoulder. "I'll pray to the God above that you don't die!"

As the city official walked off and left him to his own devices, Kieran began to think about his target and what to do next; folding the parchment and tucking it securely into his pocket, Kieran felt a surge of anticipation. He had found his next quest, and it seemed like it'd be a good challenge for him.

As the sun began to set, casting a warm golden glow over the town, Kieran headed toward the local inn to rest and prepare for the journey ahead. His mind buzzed with excitement and his heart brimmed with determination.

Tomorrow would bring a new chapter in his adventures—a chapter filled with challenges, rewards, and the promise of growth.

With a steely resolve, Kieran knew that he was ready for whatever awaited him. The Shadow would be no match for him in the end, he knew that much, but each person he hunted was unique in their abilities and ways of defying him.

For that, the minty blue bounty hunter knew that there would be challenges along the way that he'd had to carefully consider and outsmart, but he had an unshakable faith in himself and what he was capable of.

The Highland Plains had been just the beginning, a mere taste of the grand tapestry of Arthos that lay before him. With each mission, he would weave his own story, leaving a trail of bravery and resilience in his wake.

And so, as the sun dipped below the horizon, Kieran embraced the unknown, ready to face the trials and triumphs that awaited him on his path. The world of Arthos beckoned, and he was more than willing to answer its call.

The door swung open with a creak as Kieran stepped into the dimly lit tavern, the soft murmur of voices and the warm aroma of hearty meals filling the air. His keen eyes scanned the rustic interior, the flickering candlelight casting dancing shadows on the wooden beams and worn furniture. Weary from his travels, he sought solace in the embrace of the familiar atmosphere.

Finding an unoccupied spot at the aged wooden counter, Kieran lowered himself onto a stool and let out a sigh, the tension of the day slowly ebbing away.

He ran his fingers through his minty blue fur, his gaze fixed on the assortment of light blue glassware and bottles lining the shelves behind the barkeep.

The tavern's lively patrons, lost in their conversations and laughter, formed an almost comforting backdrop to Kieran's thoughts. He beckoned the bartender, a robust swift fox woman with a friendly grin, and ordered his favorite whiskey—a drink that never failed to bring warmth to his heart and clarity to his mind.

"Surely, surely, order coming right up, sir," the swift fox looked him over for a moment with curiosity, seemingly analyzing his attire. "I recognize that type of clothing. Here to save the day, bounty hunter?" she said with a giggle.

Kieran stared at her with a subtle smile. "Yep."

The bartender winked at him. "I won't bother telling you to be careful, you look well and fit enough for the job, mister...?" She trailed off, inviting him to introduce himself to her.

"Kieran," he raised his hand up and then back down to the counter. "Kieran Dravenholm."

"I'm Isabella," she responded warmly. "Nice to meet you, mister Dravenholm."

Kieran nodded curtly, not quite in his element as he socialized with the swift fox girl. "You too."

As the bartender busied herself with Kieran's order, a sudden ripple of excitement seemed to sweep through the tavern. Curious, Kieran glanced toward the source of the commotion and caught sight of an unexpected presence. A short dark blue fox girl, her ethereal aura setting her apart from the crowd, had entered the tavern accompanied by a small, fiery dragon perched on her shoulder.

Kieran's interest was piqued as he observed the celestial fox girl, her vibrant jade-green eyes scanning the room with a mix of curiosity and confidence. The intricate patterns of her wings hinted at a story untold, an otherworldly elegance that intrigued him. She also wore a pair of fancy, gold-colored goggles atop her head.

With a sense of intrigue, Kieran's gaze lingered on the girl's companion—a diminutive fire dragon, its flickering flames casting a warm and comforting glow around them. It was a sight both mesmerizing and enchanting, as if a slice of a magical realm had materialized within the walls of the tavern.

Both of them seemed to ignore all the eyes staring at them.

As fate would have it, their paths converged as the celestial fox approached the counter. Kieran's gaze met hers, and a subtle recognition passed between them—a shared understanding of the mysteries that lurked beneath the surface of their respective journeys.

She was not a local, she was a traveler just like him. Judging by what she was wearing, Kieran thought she might also be some kind of bounty hunter like him.

'But... she's so small,' he reasoned with mild concern. 'Could she really be a bounty hunter?' With a gracious smile, the celestial fox took a seat beside Kieran, her presence radiating an energy that seemed to light up the space around her. "A drink for the weary traveler," she quipped, face-planting onto the counter with a hand raised for the bartender.

Her little dragon looked at Kieran curiously, gently sniffing at him from a distance. Kieran's lips curved into a faint smile. "You seem like you've traveled quite a distance," he replied, his curiosity piqued by the starry aura that seemed to envelop her.

The girl chuckled softly, her gaze playful yet genuine. "You could say that. The road has its surprises, doesn't it?"

Kieran's eyes widened for a moment in agreement. "Indeed, it does."

Their conversation flowed effortlessly due to the two sharing a wavelength, a mixture of anecdotes and shared experiences exchanged over glasses of spirits. The tavern's ambiance seemed to shift, the world outside fading as a newfound connection took root. They learned each other's names, and Kieran did quite like hers; it was Tessa Hawthorne.

Tessa ordered a vodka for herself, which was surprising for the bounty hunter given her size and gender. "Isn't that strong for you?" Kieran asked.

"N-no," she said through coughs as she sipped. "It burns, yeah, but I like the tougher things because they help harden me. It tastes really good too, though! It's got orange and cranberry in it, my favorite flavors."

Kieran gripped his whiskey glass and swirled the liquid around in a circular motion. "If you say so."

A moment later, Tessa beckoned for the bartender again who came over with ears perked attentively. "Hi, yea, I'd like to order a flame-brand tequila, if you've got it, ma'am."

Kieran had been taking a sip of his whiskey when she said this and he damn near spat it out at hearing this.

"Yes, miss, I'll get that for you as soon as I can," Isabella said politely, but no doubt thinking the same thing as the minty blue fox. This was proven when the swift fox and Kieran locked eyes with each other in concern for a moment before she went off to fulfill the order.

Kieran could not get out any words and just stared at Tessa with shock.

She glanced at him, smiling, beginning to pet her fire dragon. "What?"

"Um," Kieran raised a brow. "I mean to each their own. You are one tough apple pie." He took another swig, looking away from her.

Tessa giggled, honestly rather cutely. "Oh, that's not for me, silly!" she said, scratching under her dragon's chin. "That's for Perseus."

"Perseus?"

"My dragon."

Perseus, her little fire dragon, looked over at Kieran and seemed to carefully watch him. Now that he thought about it, Tessa's pet had been staring at him the whole time as if on guard, often out of the corner of his eye.

"Wait, wait... your dragon... drinks?" Kieran asked quietly. "I heard that correctly?"

Perseus wagged his tail much like a dog at his question.

Tessa nodded. "He likes it spicy."

Kieran's astonishment slowly morphed into a mixture of amusement and disbelief.

He shook his head and let out a hearty chuckle. "Well, I've seen my share of unusual sights in this world, but a dragon that enjoys tequila is definitely a new one. Perseus, huh? Quite the fiery companion you have there."

Tessa beamed with pride, her eyes sparkling as she continued to pet Perseus affectionately. "Oh, he's not just fiery in taste preferences. He's got quite an adventurous spirit too. We've been through more escapades than I can count. Right, Perseus?"

The dragon responded with an enthusiastic chittering sound, almost as if agreeing with her. Kieran couldn't help but be charmed by the dynamic duo before him. He extended a hand towards Perseus, offering a friendly gesture to the little fire creature.

"He's quite the character," Kieran noted, a playful glint in his eyes. "And I have to admit, you've piqued my curiosity. A flame-brand tequila for a dragon, huh? That's a tale to remember."

As Isabella returned with the drink, placing it carefully on the bar, Kieran leaned back and raised his glass in a toast. "To new acquaintances, unexpected friendships, and the mysteries of a world that keeps surprising us."

Tessa's eyes sparkled as she clinked her glass against his, and even Perseus seemed to join in the celebration with a little burst of flames over his tequila that illuminated the cozy tavern corner. He carefully took polite sips of his drink, the fire not harming him at all.

Kieran was sure that the dragon was immune to fire damage, which honestly made sense. Perseus could likely stick his head in the flaming brew and not be hurt, but then he'd look silly...

and well, the tavern would suffer immense damages due to the fire overflowing the mug.

The three of them, an eclectic group brought together by chance, shared a moment of camaraderie that felt as warm as the drink they enjoyed.

As the night rolled on and the tavern bustled with activity, Kieran found himself engrossed in lively conversation with Tessa.

Her tales of daring escapades and mischievous exploits from all around the vast and expansive world of Arthos were nothing short of captivating, and he couldn't help but admire the fearless spirit that seemed to radiate from her every word.

It was refreshing, a welcome break from the often solitary life he led. He of course loved his isolation but once in a while, a pause was more than enjoyed.

Perseus had nestled comfortably on Tessa's shoulder, occasionally emitting playful sparks that danced in the air. The little guy could even emit specially shaped sparks, such as hearts, plants, and objects.

Kieran couldn't help but chuckle at the creature's antics, finding himself genuinely amused by the dynamic between Tessa and her fiery companion.

As time grew ever later, Kieran noticed a subtle shift in the tavern's atmosphere. The air seemed to grow tense, and he caught sight of patrons exchanging furtive glances and hushed whispers. Instinctively, his senses sharpened, and he discreetly shifted his gaze around the room, trying to discern the cause of the unease.

It wasn't long before his attention was drawn to a newcomer who had entered the tavern. A tall figure, cloaked in shadows, moved with a purposeful stride.

Kieran's sharp eyes caught a glimpse of scars that marred the stranger's form, a testament to battles fought and survived.

There was an air of intrigue and danger surrounding the newcomer, an aura that seemed to demand attention.

The stranger's gaze swept across the room, and for a brief moment, their eyes locked. Kieran felt a chill run down his spine, a feeling that was both thrilling and unnerving. It was then that he noticed the glint of recognition in the stranger's eyes, a flicker of something that sent a shiver of foreboding through him.

Tessa, caught up in her animated storytelling, seemed oblivious to the tension that had settled over the tavern. Perseus, however, emitted a low growl, his small form tensing on Tessa's shoulder, which caused her to pause and pay attention. Kieran's hand instinctively moved to the hilt of his weapon, his senses on high alert.

The stranger continued to make their way through the tavern, the atmosphere seemingly shifting in their wake. Kieran's mind raced, thoughts and possibilities swirling as he tried to piece together the puzzle before him.

He couldn't shake the feeling that this newcomer, with their scars and enigmatic presence, was no ordinary traveler. As the stranger approached the bar, Kieran's gaze remained fixed, his instincts urging him to stay vigilant. He exchanged a quick glance with Isabella, who had also noticed the newcomer's arrival.

There was an unspoken understanding between them, a shared recognition of the potential danger that lingered in the air.

Kieran's grip on his drink tightened, his focus unwavering as he awaited the next turn of events. In this corner of the tavern, where tales of adventure and camaraderie had been shared just moments ago, an undercurrent of uncertainty now simmered.

Isabella subtly positioned herself closer to Kieran, her eyes never leaving the stranger. The atmosphere had shifted from one of joviality to one of caution, like the calm before a storm. The tavern's patrons seemed to sense the change as well, conversations dwindling into hushed murmurs.

The stranger's presence at the bar seemed deliberate, yet there was an air of mystery that clung to them. Their gaze swept over the patrons, lingering on each face as if searching for something—or someone.

Kieran's keen instincts told him that this wasn't a mere chance encounter. There was intent behind those scarred eyes, a motive that had brought them to this seemingly ordinary tavern.

The tension in the air was palpable, a silent stand-off between the stranger and those who had taken notice of their arrival. Kieran's mind raced, evaluating every possible scenario. He had faced danger countless times before, but there was something about this situation that felt different.

As if in response to the unspoken tension, the tavern's door swung open once again. Another figure entered, one whose presence seemed to amplify the charged atmosphere. A dark green colored male corsac fox.

Kieran's eyes narrowed as he observed the newcomer, his instincts urging him to remain vigilant. The green fox's gaze swept over the tavern, his gray eyes locking onto the stranger at the bar.

There was a flicker of recognition, a momentary connection that spoke of shared history.

Tessa tensed beside Kieran, her fingers curling around the hilt of a concealed blade.

The stranger finally turned away from the bar, their purpose seemingly fulfilled. With a final glance around the tavern, they made their exit, leaving behind an aura of mystery that lingered like a whisper in the wind.

Kieran gave Isabella a questioning look, wondering if she knew anything about what this all meant. Tessa's gaze remained fixed on the door, a mix of determination and curiosity in her eyes.

Isabella sighed softly, her fingers tracing the rim of her glass as she leaned closer to Kieran, her voice dropping to a conspiratorial tone. "That's

Lysander Thornwood, as mysterious as they come," she whispered. "He's been a regular in this place for longer than I can remember. Keeps to himself mostly, and doesn't engage in much conversation. But when he does, it's like every word he says carries a weight."

Tessa's grip on her blade relaxed slightly, her gaze shifting from the door to Isabella and Kieran. "Who is he? And why did he come here?"

Isabella shrugged, her gaze thoughtful. "No one knows. Some say he's a traveler, others whisper about him being involved in things best left untouched. But he's never caused any trouble, at least not directly."

As they spoke, the green-colored fox seemed to have found his way over to their corner. His scars were less intimidating up close, and his voice, though rough, carried an unexpected warmth as he greeted the group. It appeared that his presence had scared off that Lysander guy, so Kieran and Tessa instantly felt mostly relaxed around him.

Perseus, however, maintained a cautious distance, his eyes fixed on the stranger with an almost comical intensity.

Kieran observed the scene with a mixture of wariness and intrigue. "Looks like he's making himself at home," he said to Isabella humorously.

Isabella nodded, a wry smile playing on her lips. "He has a certain charm, in his own way."

Kieran shifted his attention to the green fox as he began to introduce himself to Tessa. "Hello, miss. My name is Malachai," he smiled, a blush coming over his face. "Y-you're quite pretty there.

Who might you be?" His shy smile and friendly demeanor were a stark contrast to the scars that adorned his body.

Tessa's guard remained partially up, her hand still resting on her concealed blade, but she couldn't help but be intrigued by the enigmatic stranger. Tessa's gaze met Malachai's as he introduced himself, his words stumbling slightly as a faint blush tinted his cheeks.

His genuine compliment caught her off guard, and for a moment, she was at a loss for words. She cleared her throat, a hint of a smile tugging at the corners of her lips.

"I'm Tessa," she replied, her tone cautious yet not unfriendly. "And this is Perseus," she added, gesturing to the small fire dragon who was eyeing Malachai with a mix of curiosity and wariness.

Kieran's lips twitched with amusement as he took a sip of his drink, watching the interaction unfold. "Seems like you've made an impression, Tessa."

Tessa shot him a playful glare before turning her attention back to Malachai. "So, Malachai, what brings you to Dawnbreak?" she inquired, her curiosity getting the better of her.

Malachai's eyes sparkled with a mixture of bashfulness and genuine interest. "Just passing through, really. Heard this place had a certain charm to it." His gaze shifted to Kieran, a question in his eyes. "And you, sir? Are you locals?"

Kieran leaned back in his seat, a half-smile on his lips. "I'm Kieran, and you could say that. We've been around these parts before."

Was that true? No, because this was the first time he'd visited this city, but he knew better than to seem like a new tourist in an unfamiliar environment.

It was a rule he lived by, never showing any kind of vulnerability to strangers. It kept him safe often; confidence and knowledge were key, and if those were not present then he could become a tempting target for mediocre criminals.

As the conversation continued, Kieran found himself both intrigued and wary of Malachai. His attempts at friendly banter were endearing, and he appreciated the effort he was making to connect. He noticed Tessa became increasingly more tense as well. She seemed to be enjoying herself, yet there was a guardedness in her demeanor, a reminder of the dangers that existed beyond the tavern walls.

Malachai talked with Isabella some, and with other men at the tavern, having a hearty old time. Malachai's attempts at conversation with Tessa grew more frequent and his smile more genuine. He seemed to genuinely enjoy their company.

Malachai gestured to the swift fox to order his drink, his gaze fixed on the array of bottles behind the counter. "I'll have a glass of moonberry wine, please," he requested with a polite smile.

Isabella nodded and began to prepare his drink, pouring a deep purple liquid into a glass. Malachai's fingers tapped idly on the counter as he waited, his eyes wandering around the tavern. It was clear that he was not quite used to being the center of attention, despite his attempts at friendly conversation.

When the glass of moonberry wine was placed before him, Malachai offered a grateful nod to the bartender before turning back to Tessa and Kieran. "Cheers," he said, lifting the glass in a silent toast before taking a sip.

Tessa watched him carefully, her curiosity piqued by his choice of drink. Moonberry wine was known for its sweet and slightly tart flavor, a favorite among those who appreciate a more refined taste. It was a choice that added to the enigma of his character, a complex blend of scars and subtlety.

Kieran's observant eyes flickered between Tessa and Malachai, catching the subtle shifts in body language and the play of expressions. The tavern's warm glow painted a cozy backdrop, casting an almost ethereal light on the scene unfolding before him.

Malachai's scarred visage softened as he leaned in slightly, his gaze fixed on Tessa with a mix of genuine interest and a hint of shyness. His words flowed like a gentle stream, each sentence carefully chosen as if he were navigating uncharted waters. "You know, Tessa, I've been coming to this tavern for a while now," he began, his voice a smooth undertone amidst the tavern's lively chatter. "But I must admit, I've never seen someone as captivating as you."

Tessa's reaction was a study in contrasts. Her cheeks tinged with a faint blush, a response she couldn't quite hide. At the same time, her tomboyish demeanor shone through as she playfully rolled her eyes, her lips curling into a half-smile.

"Flattery will get you nowhere, Mr. Malachai," Tessa teased, her voice carrying a hint of amusement. "I'm not so easily charmed."

Malachai's lips curled in a genuine smile, revealing a side of him that Kieran hadn't quite expected. There was a vulnerability in his eyes, a silent plea for a chance to connect, even amidst his attempts at flirtation.

Kieran's grip on his drink tightened slightly, a mixture of protectiveness and intrigue stirring within him. He watched as Malachai leaned back, his tone shifting to a more casual note.

"Well, I won't deny that I'm a regular around here," Malachai admitted, his fingers tracing the rim of his wine glass. "But it's not often that I meet someone who can match my wit and fiery spirit."

Tessa's laughter danced through the air, a clear indication that the malachite green-furred fox's words had struck a chord. Kieran couldn't help but chuckle under his breath, impressed by Malachai's ability to hold his own in this playful exchange.

A while passed, and the two kept chatting; Kieran couldn't shake off the feeling that beneath Malachai's scars and enigmatic demeanor, there was a genuine longing for connection.

The subtle flirtation was probably just a surface layer, a way for Malachai to bridge the gap between his world and Tessa's.

When Malachai's friendly advances began to take a markedly affectionate, even sensual turn, Tessa's smile faltered. The green fox had begun rubbing her back, inching closer to her, and the final straw for the starry girl was when Malachai put his hand on her thigh.

Perseus had been uncomfortable the entire time, and this was what caused the fire dragon to snap; he roared and blew a few flames at his owner's would-be suitor.

She gently but firmly turned away the excited male's attempts at closer proximity, her gaze unwavering. "I appreciate the company, Malachai, but let's keep things friendly."

Tessa stroked Perseus' neck, attempting to calm down a still grumbly dragon.

Malachai's smile remained, though there was a hint of disappointment in his eyes. "Of course, Tessa. Just thought I'd try my luck."

Tessa offered him a small, reassuring smile. "Luck has a way of surprising us sometimes."

Kieran watched the exchange between Tessa and Malachai, a subtle smirk tugging at the corner of his lips. It was clear that Malachai's advances hadn't quite hit the mark with the celestial fox girl, despite his charming attempts.

Kieran couldn't help but admire Tessa's straightforwardness and confidence in setting boundaries.

As the conversation settled and Malachai excused himself to the bathroom, Kieran decided it was time for him to retire for the night as well. He finished the last sip of his whiskey, feeling its warmth spread through him. "Well, it's been an eventful evening, but I think it's time for some shut-eye," he announced, stretching his arms above his head.

Isabella nodded in understanding. "Of course, Kieran. I can arrange a room for you if you'd like."

"That would be much appreciated," Kieran replied with a grateful smile. He glanced back at Tessa and Perseus. "You two take care now."

With a nod of farewell, he followed Isabella upstairs to the second floor, where all of the tavern's rooms were located.

Kieran was assigned a room at the end of the hall. "This is your room, I figured you were the type to like your privacy," she smiled.

"Thank you," Kieran said and handed her some gold coins. "Will five gold coins be enough?"

"Oh you only owe me two coins," she giggled, handing three pieces back to him.

Kieran held up his hand, gesturing for her to stop. "Nah, you keep the rest, you served us well tonight."

The swift fox brightened up and looked quite grateful, and then left him in peace.

CHAPTER TWO

PROTECTOR

Kieran's eyes snapped open from his otherwise restful sleep, his senses immediately on high alert. He was accustomed to the sounds of the night, the creaking of taverns settling, the distant hoot of an owl, but something was off.

A gut feeling churned within him, an unease that he couldn't ignore.

The experienced bounty hunter was seldom wrong, if ever, about the warnings his insides gave him, so he chose to listen to its whisper heedfully.

Pushing the blankets aside, Kieran quietly rose from his bed and moved to the door.

He paused for a moment, his ears straining to catch any unusual sounds from the hallway. And then he heard it—a faint whimper, a muffled protest.

A female voice!

Nothing about it could be mistaken as consensual. His heart clenched with a sudden fear, and without a second thought, he moved swiftly toward the source of the noise.

As he reached the room, a few doors down from his own, his hand instinctively went for the hilt of his blade.

He could sense that something was very wrong. Readying himself for a fight if need be, he pushed the door open and stepped inside.

The sight that met his eyes made his blood run cold. Tessa was there, her back against the wall, her expression a mix of fear and confusion.

Malachai stood before her, his demeanor predatory, his fingers reaching for her erotic areas. Kieran's heart pounded in his chest, his masculine protective instincts kicking into overdrive.

"Get away from her," Kieran's voice was low and dangerous, his gaze locked onto Malachai's.

Malachai turned to face him, his eyes narrowing with a mixture of surprise and annoyance. "Well, well, Kieran. Didn't expect you to interrupt our little moment."

Tessa's eyes flickered with relief as she saw Kieran, and she quickly stepped back from Malachai. "Kieran..."

Ignoring Malachai's taunts, Kieran took a step forward, his stance radiating a silent threat. "I don't know what you think you're doing, Malachai, but it ends right now."

Malachai's lips curled into a cruel smile, his white fangs bared in raw aggression. Without warning, he lunged at Kieran with a black dagger that had been concealed up till then, his movements fueled by a mix of rage and arrogance, but Kieran was ready, his reflexes honed by years of danger.

He sidestepped Malachai's attack and swiftly disarmed him, sending the blade clattering to the floor.

"You picked the wrong person to mess with," Kieran's voice was laced with cold fury as he pinned Malachai against the wall.

The malachite-colored fox struggled against Kieran's grip, his face contorted with anger. "You think you can protect her? You don't even know what she's capable of! You damn fool!" he roared.

Kieran's gaze remained steady, his grip unyielding. "I know enough. I won't let anyone harm her."

With a final warning glare, Kieran released Malachai, who ran out of the room as quickly as he could and turned his attention to Tessa. She looked shaken, her eyes wide with a mix of emotions. She was already crying. Without a word, he held out his hand to her, offering her the support she needed. "Tessa, are you alright?"

Tessa nodded, her voice barely above a whisper. "Yeah... t-thanks to y-y... y-you."

Kieran's gaze softened, his hand gentle as he brushed a strand of hair from her face. "Just promise me you won't leave your drink unattended ever again."

Tessa managed a small smile, her fingers lacing with Kieran's. "I won't. I... he..."

Before she could finish the sentence, a very loud commotion was heard downstairs, as if a fight had broken out.

Kieran took Tessa down with him, keeping himself between the violence and his female friend, not content to leave her alone at that time but still wanting to keep tabs on what was going on.

It turned out that after Malachai had bolted, he staggered out of the room and into the tavern's larger space. And there, waiting for him with eyes ablaze was Perseus. The fire dragon had roused from his slumber, perhaps somehow also induced by whatever drug the green fox had given to Tessa. His instincts were very attuned to the disturbance that had unfolded upstairs.

Perseus wasted no time. With a powerful lunge and deep roar, he pounced on Malachai, his sharp claws digging into the rapist's clothing and his jaws snapping dangerously close to Malachai's jugular vein. Perseus would not play nice or merciful, he had made it clear that he was Tessa's protector and he would kill without question to achieve this goal.

Kieran simply watched, with a high Tessa closely near him. He was touched by the devotion that the little dragon had for his owner.

The scene was chaotic, a whirlwind of fury and adrenaline as the fire dragon exacted his form of justice upon the man who had manipulated his beloved friend. Perseus and Malachai were locked in a fierce struggle.

The fire dragon's claws were embedded in the green fox's body, his tail thrashing, and his growls a symphony of pure hate. Malachai, on the other hand, was trapped beneath the weight and ferocity of the angered creature.

Amid the chaos, as Perseus lunged at Malachai with fierce determination, the fire dragon's jaws snapped shut just inches from Malachai's outstretched arm.

With a swift and calculated movement, Malachai managed to grab Perseus by the scruff of his neck, his gloved hand tightening around the scales despite the searing heat that radiated from the fiery creature.

A guttural growl of pain escaped Malachai's lips as the intense heat burned through his gloves and into his skin, but his determination was unshaken. With a strength that belied his lean frame, he lifted Perseus off the ground, his muscles straining against the fiery resistance of the dragon.

The dragon glowed brighter and hotter by the moment, and he jerked violently in what Kieran could only assume was rage that just kept on building.

The minty blue fox's heart raced as he realized the dire situation – if Perseus managed to break free, the consequences could be catastrophic for the tavern, and Isabella did not deserve that. Dawnbreak did not deserve that.

"Perseus, stop!" Kieran's voice rang out, his eyes locked onto Malachai's burning determination. "Let him go!"

"Perseus, no! Leave it!" Tessa yelled, her drugged state slowly losing effect due to the adrenaline pumping through her body, her eyes wide with panic as she took in the dangerous standoff.

With a final surge of effort, Malachai managed to toss Perseus aside, the fire dragon crashing into a table with a resounding crash. Ignoring the burns on his hand and the singed fabric of his clothing, as well as the blood that streamed down his slender body, the green-furred fox pushed himself to his feet and made a break toward the exit, leaving a trail of smoke and sparks in his wake.

Perseus, momentarily stunned by the impact, shook himself off and let out a furious roar that seemed to shake the very foundations of the tavern. With an agile leap, he sprang back to his feet and charged after Malachai, his fiery form beaming with unchecked hatred as he launched himself into the night.

Kieran moved quickly to Tessa's side, helping her to steady herself as she swayed on her feet. "Are you okay?"

Tessa nodded, her gaze locked on the open tavern door where Perseus had disappeared. "I have to go after them."

Kieran's jaw set with determination as he looked at Tessa, his resolve matching hers. "No.

You don't. I will." Given Tessa's personality, normally she might have argued that she was fully capable of dealing with this problem herself, but the serious weight of what had happened made her yield to him.

She nodded and sat down on the stony floor, her back against the counter perimeter.

"What the hell is going on?" screeched a confused voice.

'Isabella,' Kieran thought.

The swift fox looked petrified and scanned the tavern for information. She saw the mess, the chairs that were tossed about, the char from Perseus' attacks, and the crimson blood that lay drying. "What..." she murmured to herself.

Kieran put his hand over Isabella's shoulder. "Malachai drugged Tessa here. I caught them in the act upstairs. I beat him, and he ran down here where Tessa's dragon attacked him. He ran out after that, and her dragon pursued him," he explained in summary.

Isabella was speechless. She gasped at the news and put a hand over her mouth.

Kieran looked into Isabella's deep purple eyes. "Please, take care of Tessa for me," he said firmly. "Get a hold of the authorities."

"Surely!" Isabella said, crouching down to inspect the starry night-colored fox for injury. Tessa was silent, likely in shock and very anxious.

With that, Kieran headed back upstairs to get properly dressed, and while he was on his way Isabella called out to him. "Where are you going?"

Kieran didn't look back or stop, he only growled resolutely.

"I'm going to get that son of a bitch, and bring back the girl's dragon."

The moon's soft glow filtered through the window, casting a silvery light across the room as Kieran donned his weapons – his trusty daggers and a sleek bow slung over his shoulder. He swiftly made his way down the stairs again, an air of staidness adorning him.

Isabella looked at him while tending to Tessa, having put a soft, warm blanket over her for comfort, her eyes reflecting a mix of worry and gratitude. "Be careful, Kieran. Malachai is dangerous."

A grim smile tugged at the corner of Kieran's lips. "Dangerous works both ways," he replied cryptically before heading toward the door. As he stepped into the night, the cool air rushed over him, energizing his senses. The trail left by Perseus and Malachai was faint but discernible – scorch marks on the ground and the faint smell of burnt wood guided his way, as well as the blood splatters left behind by the mauled fox.

The chase was on, and Kieran's heart pounded with a mix of rush and resolve. He knew the risks that lay ahead, the darkness that Malachai represented, as he had seen men like him before,

and the unpredictable nature of Perseus. But he was driven by a need to make things right, to ensure Tessa's safety, and to bring an end to the chaos that had erupted in the tavern.

With each step, his determination grew stronger. The moon's light illuminated his path, casting long shadows that seemed to dance alongside him as he pursued his quarry. The night was far from over, and Kieran was prepared to face whatever challenges lay ahead in his pursuit of justice and the safety of those he cared for.

He moved with a predator's grace through the darkened cityscape. His keen senses were attuned to every sound, every rustle of leaves, every sound upon the road, and every shift in the night breeze as well as every scent it carried with it.

The trail led him deeper into the outskirts of Dawnbreak, where the shadows seemed to thicken and the air grew heavy with tension.

It was then that Kieran's sharp ears caught a distant rumble, a sound that seemed out of place in the quiet of the gloomy blackness. As he moved closer, the source of the noise became clear – a low, guttural growl that reverberated through the air.

Following the ominous sound, Kieran's steps quickened until he reached a small clearing. Kieran's heart pounded in his chest as he approached the clearing, his every instinct on high alert.

Moonlight painted an eerie tableau before him, casting long, ghostly shadows that danced across the ground.

Two imposing figures were locked in a deadly dance, a battle of wills.

His eyes widened as he took in the scene before him. One of the figures was unmistakably Perseus, now transformed into a huge fire drake, twice the size of a horse.

The other was very likely Malachai. The creature's scales blazed with an intensity that illuminated the entire area. The other figure, however, was less familiar, a dark silhouette that struggled against the might of the fire drake.

Kieran's grip on his weapons tightened as he tried to make sense of the situation. He couldn't deny the surge of protective instinct that washed over him, fueled by the knowledge that Perseus was involved.

But, how had Perseus shifted his form like that?

As he watched, Perseus unleashed a ferocious roar that seemed to shake the very ground beneath Kieran's feet. Flames seemed to boil through Perseus' maw as if charging up for a powerful, executioner attack.

Time seemed to slow as Kieran assessed the situation, his gaze flickering between the fiery chaos and the prone figure of Malachai. He couldn't deny the surge of conflicted emotions that welled up within him.

A part of him wanted to let the fire drake have his vengeance, to allow Perseus to unleash his fury upon the monster who had caused so much turmoil, but Kieran was a bounty hunter, a guardian of justice; it would be better to get information out of the fox.

With a determined exhale, he took a step forward, his voice ringing out in a clear and authoritative command.

"Perseus, enough!" Kieran's voice cut through the chaos, carrying the weight of his intent. The fire drake hesitated, his blazing eyes fixing on Kieran as if assessing him. Kieran met that fiery gaze head-on, his stance unwavering.

Maybe the bounty hunter was brave, and maybe he was very stupid; probably both, honestly. "If we take him alive, we can get more information out of him."

For a tense moment, the clearing was cloaked in a heavy silence. Perseus held Malachai captive in his burning gaze, their surroundings charged with tension.

And then, as if sensing Kieran's sincerity, the fire drake slowly released his grip, allowing Malachai to slump to the ground.

Kieran approached cautiously, keeping a watchful eye on both of them. He extended a hand toward Perseus, his voice soothing. "Good boy. Stand down."

The fire drake rumbled softly, his flames flickering as he regarded Kieran with a mixture of wariness and loyalty. Kieran turned his attention to Malachai, his expression pure, seething hostility.

Malachai's defiant gaze met Kieran's, the fire in his eyes flickering with a treacherous intensity. Kieran's patience was wearing thin, his anger simmering just beneath the surface. He had little sympathy for a troublemaker like Malachai, and his focus was solely on preventing any further chaos.

"Don't play the victim here!" Kieran snapped, his voice cutting through the tension. "You brought this on yourself, and now you're going to face the consequences."

Malachai's lips curled into a bitter smirk, his tone dripping with sarcasm like a bitter poison. "Oh, forgive me if I don't shed a tear for that dumb star-mutt."

Kieran's fists clenched at his sides, his jaw tightening. "You're a real piece of work, you know that?" he retorted, his voice a low growl. "You terrorized this place, drugged an innocent girl, and thought you could just walk away?"

Malachai's gaze never wavered, his insolence unyielding. "I did what I had to do to survive. You wouldn't understand."

"Survive?" Kieran scoffed. "Seriously, bud, you don't need sex to survive. It's but a luxury."

"F-fu..." Malachai winced in pain due to his wounds and burns. "Fuck you, man!"

The two foxes stayed locked in a tense standoff, the weight of their choices and actions hanging heavily in the air between them. Kieran's patience had run its course, and he was prepared to make sure Malachai faced the ramifications of his reckless behavior.

"Get up," Kieran commanded, his voice cutting through the silence like a blade. He withdrew his menacing dagger, ready to use if he was forced to. "We're taking you to the authorities, and you're going to answer for what you've done."

"You don't know what you're doing, boy."

"Get. Up." Kieran growled more intensely now.

The defeated malachite-colored corsac fox pushed himself off the ground with a mixture of pain and reluctance, dried blood detailing his body, his gaze never leaving Kieran's.

As they began to make their way back toward the tavern, Kieran's grip on Malachai's arm was firm and obdurate.

There would be no escape this time.

As they walked back, a hush seemed to settle over the city. The moon cast long shadows, playing tricks on the eye. In a fleeting moment, a soft breeze whispered through street-ways, carrying with it an echo of forgotten stories and unresolved destinies.

It was as if the night itself held its breath, caught in the suspense of this encounter. Kieran's steps faltered for an instant, a strange sensation washing over him – a momentary glimpse into the intricate dance of fate and circumstance. And then, as quickly as it had come, the sensation passed. Kieran shook his head slightly, as if to clear his thoughts, and tightened his grip on Malachai's arm once more. But the night had left its mark, a reminder that even in the most determined of pursuits, the universe held its secrets close, revealing only fragments of its grand design.

'I'm always wondering about you,' thought Kieran affectionately, referring to the universe and whatever was out there. He may not believe in any deities, but he did believe in meaning. He believed in endless mysteries, and whenever things were quiet his mind slipped into thought about them.

As they continued on their path, Perseus marching alongside them, Kieran couldn't help but ponder the enigma of it all. The stars above seemed to shimmer with a knowing twinkle, as if they, too, were observers in this intricate play of light and shadow. Could they be living creatures?

Kieran, a mere mortal in the vast tapestry of existence, forged ahead, determined to uncover the truths that lay hidden in the depths of the night.

As Kieran and Malachai returned to the tavern, the scene had transformed from the chaos that had ensued earlier. The authorities, clad in intricate purple and silver armor, stood vigilant amidst the remnants of the struggle. Their presence exuded an aura of order and control, a stark contrast to the previous commotion.

Isabella was in conversation with one of the armored fox men, her expression a mix of relief and concern. Tessa sat nearby, her eyes downcast as she spoke softly with another of the guards.

Perseus went to her side immediately upon setting his sight on the dark blue fox, remained there, and did not move, his fiery presence a testament to the bond between them. He was calm now, but watchful; he did not revert to his smaller form, likely in case something unexpected happened that forced him to protect his owner again.

Kieran's arrival with Malachai didn't go unnoticed. The leader of the guards, a stern yet composed swift fox figure, stepped forward with a nod of acknowledgment. "You've done well," he stated, his voice carrying a sense of authority that demanded attention. Through the armor, Kieran could see his white fur adorned with brewed tea-colored patches.

Maybe a desaturated, light brown was a good description of the color, or perhaps a light fawn color. His eyes were an icy blue, and his age was evident by the lines under them.

Kieran's grip on the criminal's arm tightened for a moment before he released him into the custody of the guards. He regarded the armored leader with a mixture of respect and wariness. "He's all yours," the bounty hunter stated simply, his gaze unwavering.

The guard leader inclined his head, his sharp eyes studying both of the males. "We'll take it from here," he affirmed, his tone leaving no room for argument. "You've helped secure Dawnbreak tonight, and for that, we are grateful."

Before the guards left, Kieran grabbed the leader's attention back on him. "Sir, would it be possible if I can be there when you question him?" he asked.

"Why's that?"

Kieran pulled out the wanted poster of The Shadow that he'd collected earlier, and displayed it to the white-and-fawn fox. "I'm working for you now."

"Ah," he smiled, "lovely. Another young man who has no idea what he's messing with. Yes, you may be present, I give permission.

Be at the prison tomorrow at noon."

"Great. I appreciate it."

As Malachai was led away by the guards, Kieran's attention shifted to Isabella and Tessa. He approached them, his expression a mix of concern and determination. "Is everyone alright?" he inquired, his voice gilded with genuine care.

Isabella offered him a reassuring smile, though weariness tugged at the corners of her eyes. "Thanks to you, yes. We are safe."

Tessa looked up, her watery gaze meeting Kieran's. "Thank you," she whispered, her voice filled with a mix of emotions that words couldn't fully capture.

Tessa's voice wavered, her words tinged with a vulnerability that cut through the air. "I... I thought I could handle myself," she began, her voice barely above a whisper. "But tonight, I was helpless. If you hadn't come when you did..." Her voice trailed off, the unspoken words hanging heavily between them.

Kieran's expression softened, a genuine empathy radiating from his eyes. He crouched down in front of Tessa, his voice gentle. "You're not alone in this, Tessa. None of us can predict what might happen. It's not a reflection of your strength."

Tessa's breath shuddered as she wiped away a tear, her gaze dropping to the ground. "It's just... I never wanted to be a victim again. I thought I had moved past that part of my life. I'm strong... I-I just want to be strong."

Kieran's hand reached out to gently lift Tessa's chin, guiding her gaze back to his. "Tessa, you're not defined by what happened to you. You're defined by your courage, your resilience, and the person you've become." His words held an unwavering conviction as if he carried the weight of his own experiences and those of others who had faced similar trials.

Tessa's lips quivered, a mixture of gratitude and pain in her eyes. "Y-Yea..." she whispered again, her voice trembling.

Kieran offered her a reassuring smile, his hand resting on hers. "You're stronger than you know," he said, his words a quiet affirmation that echoed in the stillness of the late-night tavern.

Tessa lightly exhaled, feeling slightly better at the moment they shared, and hugged Kieran tightly. This surprised him but he leaned into it and hugged her back. He hoped she felt safe in his embrace; this is what he loved, keeping people safe and helping them heal from the wrongs done to them.

As the authorities concluded their investigation, the atmosphere in the building gradually shifted from tension to relief. Isabella and the guards worked diligently to restore a sense of normalcy, while Tessa found solace in the company of those who had stood by her side.

Through it all, Kieran remained a steady presence, a silent guardian who had woven himself into the fabric of their lives in ways they couldn't yet comprehend.

The events of the night had unraveled the threads of their initial encounter, revealing a depth of strength and vulnerability that had brought them together in unexpected ways.

Kieran had a deep-seated feeling that the echoes of this night would resonate long into the future, shaping the destinies of those touched by its shadows and its light.

CHAPTER THREE

INTERROGATOR

—★★★—

Kieran stepped into the prison building, the air within noticeably heavier than the bright daylight outside. The place had that distinct aroma of damp stone and the faint scent of despair that seemed to permeate every corner of such establishments.

He was dressed in his usual attire, a blend of rugged practicality and subtle elegance that had become his signature. The pendant around his neck caught a glimmer of light as he moved, a touch of blue fluorite to contrast against his minty fur.

The interior was dimly lit, and the echoing sounds of footsteps and muted conversations added to the ambiance. As Kieran approached the front desk, a burly fox guard with a stern expression regarded him. Kieran's gaze met his, unwavering but not confrontational.

"Can I help you?" the guard inquired, his voice gruff but not hostile.

"I'm here to meet with the guard leader about the questioning of Malachai," Kieran replied, his tone steady.

The guard's demeanor softened slightly as he recognized Kieran's purpose. "Ah, you must be Kieran. Captain Stoneclaw has been expecting you. Go down the hallway, take a right, and it's the third room on your left."

Kieran offered a curt nod of appreciation before proceeding down the corridor. The prison's interior seemed to close in on him as he walked, the weight of what this place signified settling in his chest. He reached the designated room and paused for a moment, mentally preparing himself for the encounter ahead.

With a deep breath, he pushed open the door and entered the room. The scene inside was tense, the atmosphere heavy with anticipation.

The guard leader, a figure of authority with polished armor and a stern countenance, stood by a table. Malachai was seated on the other side, his scars and his gaze equally defiant. Another guard was present alongside the two.

Kieran's entrance didn't go unnoticed. The guard leader, whom he now knew was called Stoneclaw, turned his gaze to him, a nod of acknowledgment exchanged between the two.

Kieran's eyes then met Malachai's, the unspoken tension between them almost touchable.

The rapist had had his wounds bandaged and treated, and he was now wearing a black shirt and trousers. *'He's not worth the supplies used,'* he thought bitterly.

The room was small and sparsely furnished, the dim light from a high window casting beams of light on the stone walls. Soft shapes of ivy leaves from around the windows on the outside could be seen in the form of shadows on the wall behind Malachai.

Kieran's presence felt like a ripple in the charged air, his every movement deliberate as he took a step closer to the table. He didn't say anything, letting the silence speak for itself as he prepared for the interrogation to unfold.

Kieran's piercing gaze bore into Malachai, his eyes a reflection of the storm brewing within him. The bounty hunter's posture was rigid, his stance conveying a sense of unwavering determination.

He leaned against the rough stone wall, crossing his arms over his chest as he waited for the proceedings to begin.

Malachai's colorless eyes flicked up to meet Kieran's, a mix of defiance and something else, perhaps a hint of curiosity, dancing in their depths. His scars seemed to writhe in the shifting shadows, adding an air of danger to his otherwise battered appearance. The two foxes locked together, an unspoken challenge passing between them, a silent duel of wills that spoke volumes without a single word being uttered.

Stoneclaw cleared his throat. "Kieran Dravenholm, I presume?" he asked, seemingly rhetorically.

Kieran gave a curt nod, acknowledging the guard leader's statement but offering no further pleasantries. He was here for a purpose, and he intended to see it through.

Stoneclaw continued. "Famous bounty hunter, I see. We did some digging on you."

"So they say," Kieran commented humbly.

The guard leader motioned to the cherry-wood chair opposite Malachai, a signal for Kieran to take a seat. Kieran obliged, his movements deliberate and controlled. He settled into the wooden chair, keeping his focus on the rapist the whole time.

The room seemed to hold its breath as Captain Stoneclaw took his place at the head of the table. His gaze shifted between Kieran and Malachai, his expression one of rigorous pondering. "Malachai Whitewood," he began, his voice steady, "you stand accused of actions that have caused harm and disruption within our town. Your presence here has cast a shadow of fear upon our streets."

Malachai's lips curled into a half-smirk, a flicker of amusement crossing his scarred face. "Is that so?" he replied, his tone laced with a mixture of sarcasm and nonchalance. He seemed almost proud of that fact.

Kieran's fingers tapped rhythmically against the arm of the chair, a barely perceptible sign of his growing impatience. He was here for answers, for information that could shed light on the enigma surrounding Malachai and his connection to Tessa's recent ordeal.

He needed to know what it all meant; his curiosity was strong, as well as his drive for justice as he saw fit.

The guard leader leaned forward, his gaze undeviating as he locked eyes with the malachite-furred criminal. "We want the truth, Whitewood. No bullshit, we hear it enough every day in this domicile, and we always end up getting what we want in the end anyway. Tell us everything you know about the events that transpired, and the reasons behind your actions."

Malachai looked away from the guard leader to Kieran, a subtle challenge becoming rather evident. "And why would I do that?" he retorted, his voice dripping with defiance.

Kieran's jaw clenched, his frustration simmering beneath the surface. He had come here seeking answers, seeking justice for Tessa and closure for himself. He leaned forward, his voice low and controlled. "Because if you don't, I assure you, you'll wish you had."

The room seemed to hang on a precipice, a delicate balance between impending conflict and the quest for truth. The echo of Kieran's words lingered a subtle promise that held more weight than any threat.

The guard leader was unshaken, his patience tested but not broken in the slightest.

"Whitewood, you're not in a position to be defiant," he stated firmly. "We have evidence, witnesses who saw you with the girl before she was found in a disoriented state. You can make this easier on yourself."

A tense silence settled over the room as the gravity of the situation hung heavy in the air. Malachai's fingers drummed rhythmically against the tabletop, a subtle show of his agitation. His scarred visage seemed to shift with every passing shadow, an enigma wrapped in a veil of defiance.

Kieran remained fixed on the criminal, his mind working through the layers of this puzzle. He knew there was more to this story, a hidden truth waiting to be unveiled... he had not forgotten the words Malachai had spoken about Tessa. There was more than met the eye here, this could not have been a simple horny male looking for fun with an innocent girl.

"Look," Kieran's voice softened, a note of sincerity cutting through the tension. "I've had time to think since last night. We both know you're not a mindless thug. There's a reason you're here, a reason you got involved with Tessa."

Malachai's eyes flickered, a fleeting moment of vulnerability that was quickly masked by his trademark defiance. "What makes you think I'll spill my so-called 'secrets' to the likes of you?" he sneered his words, a shield against the truth.

Kieran's fingers tapped thoughtfully against the arm of the chair, his mind racing as he sought a way to breach the walls that Malachai had erected around him. "Because," Kieran began, his voice measured and calm, "whatever your reasons were, they led you down a dangerous path. And if you're not careful, that path will lead you to a fate you can't escape."

Stoneclaw sat mostly idle for now, his presence a constant reminder of the consequences that hung over Malachai's head. "You have a choice, Whitewood," he said, his voice a blend of authority and empathy. "Cooperate, and we'll take that into consideration when the time comes."

The room seemed to hold its breath, the weight of the truth and the weight of the unknown converging in a clash of destiny. Malachai's lips curled into a sardonic smile, a flicker of amusement dancing in his eyes. "You think you're clever, don't you?" he scoffed, his voice dripping with mockery. "Coming in here, trying to play detective, thinking you can unravel my so-called 'secrets'."

Kieran's gaze remained unyielding, his suspicion only deepening. "I've seen enough to know when someone's hiding something," he replied evenly. "And you, Malachai, are hiding a lot."

The malachite-furred fox leaned back in his chair, his demeanor almost nonchalant. "Well then, by all means, enlighten me," he retorted, his tone a mixture of boredom and challenge. "Tell me what wild theories you've concocted about me."

Kieran's fingers tightened into fists, his patience wearing thin. "I don't need theories," he shot back. "I need facts. Starting with why you were so interested in Tessa in the first place."

Malachai's laughter was sharp and cutting, a sound that seemed to reverberate through the room. "Oh, Tessa," he mused, his tone dripping with false nostalgia. "She's just a means to an end, my friend. A pawn in a much larger game."

Kieran's eyes narrowed, his suspicion deepening. "And what game is that?"

Malachai leaned forward, his gaze locking onto Kieran's with an intensity that sent a shiver down Kieran's spine. "The kind of game you wouldn't understand," he replied cryptically. "But let's just say, I have my reasons for everything I do."

Kieran's jaw clenched, his frustration boiling to the surface. "Stop dancing around the truth," he growled. "You're not fooling anyone."

Malachai's smile never wavered, and was a mask of confidence that seemed unbreakable. "Oh, my dear bounty hunter," he purred, his words laced with a sinister edge. "You underestimate me. But then again, that's exactly what I want."

Kieran growled. "I've tangled with enough people like you to recognize when someone's trying to blind me," he retorted, his voice full of quiet intensity. "You can play your games, but I won't be a pawn in this twisted dance."

Malachai's chuckle was like a venomous melody, a melody that sent a chill down Kieran's spine. "Ah, but isn't life itself a dance of shadows?" he mused, his eyes glinting with a mix of amusement and something darker. "We all have our roles to play, my friend. Even you."

Kieran's fingers drummed on the table, his impatience a tangible force in the room. "Cut the philosophical nonsense," he snapped. "We're talking about lives at stake here."

Malachai's gaze flickered, a momentary crack in his mask of confidence. "Lives?" he echoed, his tone almost innocent. "Ah, yes, lives are fragile, aren't they? Easily snuffed out, like a candle in the wind."

Kieran's patience was wearing thin, his frustration simmering just beneath the surface. "Enough with the riddles," he growled. "Tell me what you know about Tessa."

Malachai leaned back, his fingers steepled as if in contemplation. "The star-furred fox," he mused, his voice a velvet whisper. "Such an intriguing girl, don't you think? But my interest in your celestial friend goes beyond mere curiosity."

Kieran's eyes narrowed, his suspicion growing sharper. "Then enlighten me," he demanded. "Why her? What do you gain from all of this?"

Malachai's smile was like a serpent's, a cunning glint in his gaze. "Power, my dear bounty hunter," he hissed. "The kind of power that transcends worlds. And Tessa, well, she's the key to unlocking that potential."

Kieran's fists clenched. "You won't succeed," he vowed. "I won't let you use her for whatever twisted plans you have."

Malachai's laughter was like shards of ice, a chilling sound that echoed in the air. "Ah, defiance," he purred. "How charming. But mark my words, Kieran, it's already too late for Tessa.

The shadows have a way of consuming even the most valiant of souls."

The room seemed to close in around them, the weight of their words hanging in the air like a storm on the horizon. As the truth continued to elude them, the search for answers deepened, casting a veil of uncertainty over them like a dark cloud.

Kieran narrowed his yellow eyes. "You speak of power, but power over what? What could be worth jeopardizing lives for?"

Malachai's eyes gleamed with a sinister light, a predatory aura enveloping him. "Ah, Kieran, you see the world in such narrow terms," he replied, his voice dripping with condescension. "Lives are but stepping stones in the grand tapestry of existence. Sacrifices must be made for the greater design."

Kieran's patience wore thin, his frustration seeping into his words. "Sacrifices? You mean you're willing to manipulate and destroy just to fulfill your own desires?"

Malachai's smile remained, his demeanor unflappable. "Desires, intentions—such trivial concepts, don't you think? My goals transcend your limited perspective."

Kieran's hands clenched into fists at his sides, his voice sharp. "Enough of your cryptic nonsense. If you think that I'll stand by while you use Tessa as some pawn, you're gravely mistaken."

Malachai's gaze bore into Kieran's, an unsettling calm in his eyes. "You're a fascinating one. Your righteous fury, your unwavering determination—it's almost poetic."

Kieran's nostrils flared, his restraint teetering on the edge. "You're like a brick wall," he grumbled, frustrated.

Malachai's laughter cut through the tension like a blade, sharp and cold. He raised his voice and leaned forward. "My dear Kieran, you're nothing more than a fleeting gust of wind in this grand design. But by all means, keep fighting. It's quite entertaining."

As the interrogation continued, Kieran's mind raced trying to decipher the layers of deception woven into the criminal's words. The dim light in the room seemed to cast eerie shadows on Malachai's face, enhancing the air of mystery that surrounded him. The bounty hunter was not trained in the skill of questioning criminals, he was more fit for bringing them in to the authorities. Despite that, this time he wanted answers; this all felt personal to him.

The guard leader leaned forward, his voice tinged with frustration. "Enough of your games, Whitewood. Give us the answers we need."

Malachai's lips curled into a sly smile, revealing his fangs, a hint of triumph in his gaze. "You underestimate the power at play here," he taunted. "You think your little realm can contain the forces that seek to break free? You don't even know what you're dealing with."

Kieran's patience wore thin, but before he could interject, the sound of hurried footsteps echoed in the corridor outside. The door burst open, revealing a frantic guard. "Sir," the guard breathed heavily, his eyes avoiding Kieran's. "We've received an urgent report. Trouble at the city gates."

Stoneclaw's brow furrowed. "What sort of trouble?"

"An ambush," the guard explained. "A group of rogue foxes, armed and dangerous. We need all hands on deck."

Stoneclaw sighed, retaining his outward confidence, but the minty blue bounty hunter could read him well. He seemed a bit overwhelmed by everything. "We have an urgent situation," he announced, his voice firm. "I'll have to leave to deal with it, but we can't afford to halt the interrogation."

Kieran's eyes narrowed slightly at the guard leader's words, a subtle unease settling in the pit of his stomach. He watched as the guard leader turned to a fox nearby. "Williams, I'm appointing you to take charge in my absence."

Williams, a stocky, long-furred male fox of a slate gray color, nodded in acknowledgment. "Of course, sir. You can count on me."

With a final nod, Stoneclaw strode out of the room, leaving Kieran alone with Williams and the enigmatic Malachai. Kieran's instincts buzzed like a warning signal, his gaze shifting between the two figures before him. He couldn't shake the feeling that something was off, that there were undercurrents of hidden motives beneath the surface.

"Let's get back to it then," Williams said, his voice seemingly steady as he turned his attention to Malachai. "You were saying something about Tessa's unique abilities."

Malachai leaned back in his chair, his posture relaxing. "Ah, yes," he drawled, his voice smooth as silk. "Tessa's abilities... a subject of fascination, indeed." He met Williams' gaze with an enigmatic look as if he held all the answers to a puzzle that had yet to be fully deciphered. "You see, my dear interrogator, Tessa is no ordinary celestial fox." Malachai's fingers tapped idly on the table, his demeanor radiating a sense of self-assuredness.

"Unlocking her power is like unraveling the threads of destiny itself," the malachite-furred fox continued, his tone almost reverent. "Imagine the influence one could wield with a force that transcends the boundaries of worlds. Such power could reshape reality itself."

Malachai's words hung in the air, a tantalizing promise of untold possibilities. His gaze never wavered, his eyes fixed on Williams as if he held the key to an intricately crafted lock. "But, of course, that's just the beginning," he concluded, nonchalantly smiling in his chair. "There are layers to Tessa's abilities that even she has yet to discover."

Williams' expression remained carefully neutral as he absorbed Malachai's words, his fingers drumming rhythmically on the coarse surface of the table. His eyes, however, betrayed a flicker of anticipation, a hunger for the secrets that Malachai dangled before him.

"Transcending boundaries and reshaping reality," Williams mused, his voice tinged with a thoughtful tone. "Indeed, a tempting prospect. But such power comes at a cost, doesn't it? And I imagine you have a plan to ensure you're the one reaping the benefits."

The stocky fox's gaze locked onto Malachai's, a silent exchange of understanding passing between them. Williams leaned in slightly, his voice dropping to a conspiratorial whisper. "Tell me, Malachai, how do you envision this unfolding? How do you plan to harness Tessa's potential for your own gain?"

Malachai sported a mischievous smirk, his nonchalance almost maddening in the face of the thick tension that gripped the room. "Ah, dear Williams," he chirped, his tone dripping with condescension. "You misunderstand. I am merely the orchestrator of a grand symphony, a humble composer of fate's melody. The true conductor, the one who will wield Tessa's potential, is someone far beyond your comprehension."

Malachai seemed to be relishing in the intrigue he had stirred with his ever-so-mysterious responses. "You see, I am but a pawn in a game played by forces much greater than you or I. The true players remain hidden in the shadows, and it is their desires that shall shape the course of destiny."

Malachai's arrogance bordered on the infuriating, a masterful display of manipulation that left a bitter taste in Kieran's mouth. As the enigmatic criminal spoke, the web of deception seemed to tighten, its intricate threads weaving a tapestry of uncertainty and foreboding.

Williams' facade of composure wavered for an instant, a flicker of doubt crossing his features. But just as quickly, he regained his steely resolve, his eyes narrowing as he met Malachai's gaze head-on. "And who might these elusive players be, Whitewood? Enlighten us, if you're so inclined."

"Maybe I will, once you prove yourself worthy of the knowledge, Williams," Malachai crossed his arms.

Kieran watched closely as the questioning session continued, his mind racing with suspicions he couldn't quite put into words. Were they even suspicions? He couldn't quite tell anymore. All he knew was that with the deficit of Captain Stoneclaw, the air had changed and he didn't like it. He couldn't put his finger on why that was the case, he simply felt it.

Then, suddenly out of nowhere, Williams suggested a break.

Kieran's eyes narrowed. The stocky gray fox was acting far too casually for Kieran's liking. A break? Right in the middle of a crucial interrogation? His fingers tightened around the arms of his chair, a surge of anticipation coursing through him.

Williams motioned for Malachai to follow. The malachite-colored fox got up without refusal, and without a word followed the guard. He limped a tad, Kieran noticed. Perseus had certainly done a number on him.

"Come back later, Kieran, we will continue then," instructed the gray fox.

The door closed behind them, the metallic click echoing in the room like a starting gunshot.

CHAPTER FOUR

ORTHODOXY

— ★ —

Kieran stood up from his chair with a controlled sense of urgency.

He couldn't shake the unsettling feeling that something was amiss. Williams' sudden decision to break off the interrogation was far from typical, and Kieran was not one to dismiss his instincts lightly.

Leaving the stifling room behind, Kieran found himself in the narrow stone corridor outside the interrogation chamber. He paused for a moment, glancing at the guards on duty, who seemed oddly impassive about the whole situation.

A decision loomed before him. Would he follow Malachai and Williams to investigate their unscheduled break, or would he take some time to collect his thoughts, far from the tension of the guardhouse? He realized he had options.

Kieran's heart yearned to confront the rogue foxes who had been causing chaos in Dawnbreak, also. This could be the moment to track them down. Yet, at the same time, there was an instinct, almost like an itch at the back of his mind, that urged him to consider the anomaly within the guardhouse.

This would take some thought.

Kieran's footsteps echoed softly in the quiet streets as he made his way to the grand Orthodox church of Dawnbreak. Its gold spires and intricate architecture loomed above him as he approached the heavy, dark oak doors.

Though he wasn't a believer in the faith practiced here, he couldn't deny the solemn tranquility that filled the air within these hallowed walls.

Pushing open the creaking doors, Kieran entered the dimly lit sanctuary. The scent of frankincense and myrrh incense hung in the air, adding to the atmosphere of contemplation and reflection. He chose a pew near the back, away from any other worshipers, as the soft chanting of a distant choir flowed around him.

The high, arched ceiling soared above, adorned with intricate frescoes that told stories of faith, sacrifice, and devotion. Kieran had no connection to these religious tales, but the artistry and history woven into every brushstroke and stone spoke to him in a way he couldn't explain.

He sat down, letting the polished wooden pew coolly embrace him. His mind was a whirlwind of thoughts and questions, doubts and suspicions.

As he dove into deep thought there, Kieran's mind drifted like motes of dust in the dim, filtered sunlight that streamed through the colorful stained glass windows. The vibrant hues and intricate patterns depicted scenes from the Orthodox faith, as well as saints who had been martyred or done something notable; but the biggest depiction in the stained glass was none other than their God, Iesu.

Again, Kieran did not believe in this God, but whenever he looked at images of Him, he couldn't help but be unable to hold eye contact for long. He'd never admit this to anyone, but the eyes of Iesu were intimidating, yet so full of gentle love at the same time.

The minty fox did not understand it, but he chalked it up to being a result of the incredible skills of the artist to depict Iesu and what makes up His caricature.

The choir's voices washed over him, soothing the restlessness in his soul. He thought about Tessa, the mysterious girl, and the looming presence of the Shadow that cast darkness over

Dawnbreak. With each passing moment, Kieran's determination to uncover the truth solidified.

The wooden pew, polished by the touch of countless hands over the years, bore the weight of his contemplation. Kieran believed in justice and truth, which at least for a moment unified him with these people. In this moment of respite within the church, he steeled himself for the battles ahead, both seen and unseen.

Lost in his contemplation, Kieran was unaware of the approach of the aged priest. He was a coal fox, fur as black as jet, with eyes that shone like the blue fluorite crystal necklace Kieran wore.

The cleric, clad in richly embroidered red and black vestments, glided quietly along the aisle. His steps were hushed, in harmony with the sacred silence enveloping the church.

Coming to a stop before Kieran, the priest offered a warm smile, the wrinkles on his face hinting at the wisdom borne of many seasons.

"Welcome, my kit," he spoke in a voice that resonated with years of comforting the troubled. "I see a storm in your eyes. Is there something that weighs upon your spirit?"

Kieran, drawn from his introspection, met the priest's gaze.

The soft glow of candlelight tinged with the crimson-colored glass of the votives, flickered in the priest's eyes, and for a moment, Kieran felt a connection—an understanding that surpassed the boundaries of belief.

He hesitated before replying, "I seek answers, Father, in a world of mysteries. There's a darkness that creeps over the world, and I aim to dispel it."

The priest nodded sagely. "In every age, heroes rise to confront the shadows. Perhaps, in seeking answers, you have already taken the first step towards dispelling the darkness. Tell me your story, young one, and perhaps together we can find the light that pierces the shadows."

Kieran sighed, and with gentle courage, he began to recount his story. He told the priest of how he had been born beneath a starless sky on a cold winter's evening.

He spoke of his training as a swordsman and the lessons that had taught him loyalty and honor in combat. He glossed quickly over the tale of his mother, father, and sister, the pain their memories brought him being too much even now.

"My parents, and little sister, were killed in a fire caused by bandits," Kieran said, his eyes almost growing somewhat dim. "Since then, I've dedicated my life to bringing these types of monsters to justice."

The priest nodded solemnly as Kieran's words sunk in. "It is admirable that you have chosen such a path," he said, "but it comes with a great cost."

Kieran nodded, "I know. I've seen things no man should ever have to—innocent people killed, lives destroyed for no good reason. And yet despite that...I can't help but feel like in some way I can make it right."

The priest nodded again in understanding. "I believe that is what it truly means to be a hero," he said, his voice taking on a more solemn tone. "To know that you can never fully make things right, but to still try despite the odds."

Kieran felt a little discouraged inside upon hearing that.

"But what about the people I can't help? What of the innocent people who suffer due to my actions?" He looked away, not wanting to see the priest's reaction.

The priest smiled and gave Kieran's shoulder a final squeeze before standing up.

"Go now," he said, "and strive to be the hero you were meant to be."

Kieran stood up slowly, feeling confident in himself and his mission. He knew what he had to do—even if it was an impossible task to fully see realized.

The priest smiled. "My name is Francis," he said warmly. "Good luck on your journey, Kieran."

Father Francis, with one last reassuring smile, bid him farewell, and Kieran took this as a sign to head out and continue on his journey. He watched as the bounty hunter made his way out of the church.

Father Francis clasped his hands together and whispered a thorough prayer for the fox's success before turning back to his meditative contemplation within the quaint church.

Deep down Kieran still felt somewhat uncertain, but at least now he knew that no matter what happened, he not only had someone in his corner but also he had solid words of advice to look back on, and to keep him going—the priest's words stayed with him long after they parted ways.

Kieran stepped out of the church and into a chill twilight. The faint half-moon had risen, casting a silver light on the weighty clouds that hung low overhead.

He looked around, ruminating in his mind for answers; he had to catch The Shadow, that was the job he had taken on and he was not about to give up. He also knew that apparently Tessa held the key to power, and was of great use to dark characters like The Shadow, and Malachai.

'Malachai...' Kieran grumbled irritably, frustrated at the thought of the man.

He had become quite critical about how the interrogation had gone. Something was fishy about it. If the minty fox didn't know any better, it was as if the guards, or at least some of them, were in cahoots with The Shadow.

The attack at the wall by rogues; was it even the truth? Could it have been a tactful ploy by corrupt individuals involved to forge what they desired?

Kieran clenched his fist as he imagined Williams smirking as he led Malachai down the hall to his cell, knowing full well that Malachai's incarceration would be overturned. Was it possible?

Kieran had learned never to doubt his sixth sense. He did not know what exactly was going on, but he knew to trust his instincts. Something was amiss, and being the adventurous, investigatory fox he was, he would get to the bottom of it all eventually.

It was so difficult knowing where to start, this case was a bit more serious than he was used to. Normally he would just have to track down a wanted man, then acquire him, and deliver him to the authorities. This time, however, while he was attempting that, many treacherous things were going on; he could just tell.

Kieran decided that he needed to find Tessa. If what was said about her was true, then she likely had more information in that somewhat absent-minded brain than he first thought.

The minty-furred fox made his way through the night, back to the tavern, hoping the celestial girl would still be there.

CHAPTER FIVE

OUT FOR COFFEE

Kieran stepped into the tavern, his boots creaking in protest as they made contact with the ancient and mismatched floor planks. The room was smokey and dimly lit; people were smoking cigars tonight, it seemed.

It smelled like vanilla and coffee beans.

'Now that's lovely,' Kieran thought, a subtle smile crossing his lips. He was tempted to deviate from his mission to sit down and enjoy one with the men, but he had to stay focused. The minty-

furred male straightened his leather clothing and continued to the bar.

Isabella did not seem to be working tonight, or if she was then she was elsewhere doing something. In her place was a gray fox girl with green eyes, dressed in a white gown. Kieran thought she was very pretty.

"Evening, Miss. I'm looking for Tessa, is she still in?"

"I just saw her, I think she went down to the local coffee shop down the road. Are you her boyfriend, or somethin'?" the gray fox chuffed.

"Nah, I'm a bounty hunter, I just need to ask her some questions," he responded, nonchalantly.

"Oh!" The gray fox girl put her palms to her mouth in shock. "Did she do somethin'? I always told Tessa that she needs to keep a low profile, gosh darn it!"

"No, no, she hasn't done anything, I just need to ask her about something she might be able to help me with," Kieran corrected gently. "Now, you have a good shift, Miss. Thank you for the help."

Kieran turned to walk out"

"Wait!"

He turned around to see the gray fox blushing and smiling. "Y-you know, I'm, uh... I'm single!"

Kieran winked at her. "I'm sure you won't have any trouble finding someone nice." With that, he headed out the door in search of Tessa.

Kieran soon found himself standing at the entrance of a cozy-looking coffee shop with an assortment of pastries in the window display. He did not know the names of the items, but he saw cookies with raspberry jellies on them, donuts with all sorts of delicious-looking toppings like powdered sugar, and cakes of many varieties.

There was almost too much for his brain to take in.

One dessert stood out to him; a cookie with chocolate pieces in it as well as chunks of white.

He had no idea what the white was supposed to be, but it intrigued him nonetheless. With intention, he ambled into the quaint coffee shop and was greeted by a waft of fresh bakery scent, causing him to salivate at the mouth.

Kieran, greeted by a comforting fusion of warmth and earthiness, felt a rush of happiness envelop him. The gentle symphony of water bubbling and the soft hum of lo-fi melodies embraced him as he scanned the room. His eyes swept across the cozy nooks adorned with flourishing plants until they settled on Tessa.

Yes! He had located her.

Before he talked with her, though, the minty fox wanted—no, needed—to get his hands on something that tasted good from this place.

Kieran strode up to the bakery section and asked the shopkeeper to grab him a vanilla cream stuffed donut; the kindly old shopkeeper obliged and handed it to him in pleasant packaging with a warm smile.

Kieran paid for it with a gold coin.

"Thank you for ordering! Have a good night, sir."

Kieran held and stared at the donut. The thing was huge and smelled like Heaven.

He delayed his gratification, as was good practice for one's benefit, until he could sit down with Tessa. He darted his eyes to where he remembered she was.

Green ivy leaves on vines draped the walls beside her.

She occupied a corner booth, a secluded sanctuary veiled by lush foliage. There, nestled against her chest, was Perseus, the small yet incredibly dangerous dragon; he was fast asleep, in all likelihood still tired from the night before dealing with Malachai. He would need rest after something like that.

In their private hideaway, they observed the ebb and flow of customers interacting with the amiable shopkeeper—a fox with yellow clothing —and contemplating the array of goods on display. The atmosphere hummed with a shared sense of community, a haven where moments unfolded in the aromatic embrace of coffee-scented air.

Kieran approached her carefully, making sure to be noticed by her afar to not startle the girl, keeping last night's events in the forefront of his mind. He was a considerate fox when he needed to be. "Hey, Tessa."

The dark blue celestial fox looked at him with her stunning green eyes. "Kieran. Hey. I hope you're doing well tonight."

Perseus blinked awake from his snooze and acknowledged the bounty hunter with a head flick and a plume of smoke that came from his nostrils, then he laid his head down to sleep again but not before a long/ feline-like stretch. The trust was there in the golden dragon's heart, and it did not go unappreciated by Dravenholm.

"I am," Kieran responded to her. "I hope you are too. I'm sorry to barge in, I just had some questions I wanted to ask."

"Oh?" her brows raised in intrigue. "About what? Also, please sit down, you're welcome to."

So far she did not seem any different than last night before the incident, but he knew that people could hide things pretty well, especially emotional things. He hoped she was alright.

Kieran obliged her request.

"So. What do you need to ask me?" Tessa looked curious.

Kieran leaned in. "Consider it that I'm on the job right now; I'm going to be professional. This is in indirect relation to last night. Can you handle that?"

He swore he could see a flash of adrenaline in the celestial fox's eyes. She paused, and lost a fair bit of her cheerfulness, as was naturally expected, but this has to be done.

"Yes."

"Okay. Good."

Kieran took a deep breath, contemplating for a moment how he would start this off. "Earlier, I was invited to the interrogation of Malachai," he began. "He claimed that you hold the key.

Tessa's expression shifted, a mixture of confusion and uncertainty. She leaned back slightly, her emerald eyes narrowing in thought.

The gravity of Kieran's question seemed to settle in, and the carefree atmosphere of the coffee shop retreated to the background.

"The key?" Tessa repeated, her voice softer, slower, more contemplative. "I... I don't know what he meant. I have talked to him before in that tavern a couple of times. He was always a bit cryptic, talking about things that felt beyond my understanding. That is why I always felt a steady level of wariness around him."

Kieran watched her closely, assessing the authenticity of her response. There was a vulnerability in Tessa's gaze, a flicker of unease that betrayed the innocence beneath her celestial facade.

"Did he ever mention anything specific, even if it seemed unrelated at the time?" Kieran probed further, his golden-yellow eyes searching for any subtle cues in Tessa's reactions.

Tessa sighed, her gaze shifting to the steaming cup of coffee in her hands. "He talked about my celestial heritage, how it made me different. I never really understood the full extent of it. He said there was power in my blood, something ancient and potent."

Kieran nodded, absorbing the information. "Did he mention anything about what your blood is capable of?"

Tessa hesitated, her eyes meeting Kieran's. "Yes, he did. He spoke about the ability to perceive things beyond this realm, but it always sounded like madness to me."

Kieran leaned back, processing the details. The puzzle pieces were scattered across the table, forming an intricate pattern, one that he was determined to figure out. "Do you feel different, Tessa? Do you have any abilities that might be considered, shall I say, otherworldly?"

Tessa's somewhat sad gaze drifted to Perseus, still slumbering peacefully by her side. "I can sense things, visions of events that haven't happened yet. But I've always thought it was just a quirk, not something of any significance."

Kieran's expression tightened. Once again, Kieran believed in spiritual things, he just did not subscribe to any particular religion; spirits, ghosts, and otherworldly abilities were completely within his realm of reality.

The celestial fox's abilities seemed to align with what Malachai hinted at, too, weaving an interesting narrative.

"Do you know what he meant by 'the key'? Anything that might unlock these powers, or perhaps something more?" Kieran pressed, urgency seeping into his tone.

Tessa shook her head, her uncertainty mirroring the complex web of the supernatural. "I wish I had answers. I truly do. But I've always been in the dark about this... this destiny."

Kieran sat back, his mind churning with the newfound revelations. The celestial fox, seemingly an ordinary denizen of Dawnbreak, now held the threads of a mysterious tapestry that connected her to dimensions and prophecies.

Kieran's gaze remained fixed on her, a furrow forming on his brow. The weight of Malachai's ominous words echoed in the quiet conversation between them.

"He said something," Kieran began, his voice measured, "when I confronted him. 'Mark my words, Kieran, it's already too late for Tessa. The shadows have a way of consuming even the most valiant of souls.' What did he mean by that?"

Tessa's expression darkened, a shadow seemingly passing over her. She traced the rim of her coffee cup with a contemplative finger as if searching for the right words in the heat rising from the brew.

"I don't know exactly," she admitted, her voice carrying a hint of unease. "But Malachai was obsessed with this notion of 'the shadows.' He believed there was a force, something beyond our understanding, that sought to consume or control those with unique abilities."

Kieran leaned forward, his gaze intense. "And he thought you were a target for this... shadow?"

Tessa nodded solemnly. "Yes. He hinted at some ancient prophecy, a destiny tied to my heritage, but I never believed in such things. It all felt like a twisted fantasy in his mind."

"Does he know something we don't?" Kieran mused quietly to himself, looking away to the side to dart between all the coffee shop customers, his mind grappling with the cryptic nature of the territory his job was taking him into.

Tessa sighed, her eyes reflecting the complexity of her emotions. There was an edge to her that struck him oddly. He'd been in this career long enough to know what it was; she was hesitating, or hiding something. She did not seem like one to do it maliciously, but he noticed.

"Tessa," he said, his voice a gentle nudge, "there's more to this, isn't there?"

Her gaze faltered for a moment before she met his eyes. "I didn't want to involve you any further... but maybe you need to know."

As she began to speak, the coffee shop transformed into a cocoon of shared confidence. Tessa's words wove a tale of her ancestry hailing from the Celestial Peaks, a lineage tied to a cosmic tapestry that transcended the boundaries of their world.

She spoke of a prophecy given by sages, ancient as time itself, foretelling a convergence of dimensions in the time of 'the end', and the emergence of one with the power to bridge the realms.

Kieran listened in a mix of awe and skepticism, grappling with the fantastical nature of the story. Yet, as Tessa continued, he saw the sincerity in her eyes, the weight of, what was for her, an inevitability that she had carried with both reluctance and acceptance.

"I was expected to fulfill this duty, to protect my home, to commune with the spirits in the other dimension," Tessa went on, growing a bit uneasy as she recounted her past, "but it was too hard. I couldn't take it anymore. Perseus helped me escape to the furthest reaches, away from my family and everything that had to do with the future they wanted for me."

The revelation settled between them, a pause in the symphony of the coffee shop. Her history was riveting.

"There are forces at play," she concluded, her voice a murmur in the quiet booth. "Forces that seek to manipulate us. That much I know is true. The prophecy, though? I can't say... and I don't care, either."

"I understand," Kieran said softly, "it seems like you just want to live free. Yet, some people seem intent on dragging you back into what you've already left far behind you."

"Yes, but that said, I don't want you to be dragged into this," Tessa said, a plea in her eyes. "It's dangerous. I've seen things, shadows that move with intent and whispers in my ears. I don't know what's real anymore. Sometimes I swear something is watching me, but I can't pinpoint anything..."

Tessa began to tear up, and Perseus woke up; the dragon quickly snuggled her. For her, it was obvious that everything was boiling over, a domino effect set by her parents and utterly shaken further by Malachai's treacherous actions.

He did not know if she was just crazy or was seeing real things, but that didn't matter nor was it his business.

Kieran's ears flattened, giving her a sympathetic look. "I don't know what Malachai or the people above him want with you exactly," he said, "but all that matters is that they do."

"Yes..."

"You will stay with me until I get to the bottom of this. I will protect you."

Tessa widened her eyes and tilted her head. "Wait, you don't need to, I have Perseus. He is more than enough to keep me safe."

Kieran shook his head. "He is a formidable warrior, but last night proved that that only goes so far."

Perseus eyed him with keen attention.

Tessa looked down, wiping her eyes. "You'd want to do this for me?"

Kieran nodded curtly. "It's not a matter of wanting to. This is a professional matter; whatever benefit you may represent to criminals, I cannot let them snag it."

"Okay... I get that, but... you're going to attract them to you. I'll bring you nothing but bad fortune."

"It doesn't matter. I've seen enough to know how to handle anything that comes my way."

Tessa grew more anxious, desperate for him to understand the weight of his decision. "You haven't seen what I have! I can't talk about all of it, but please... Kieran, just know that if you take me with you wherever you go, this case may be your last."

Kieran remained silent, sensing how upset she was.

Tessa growled and looked away, head lowered. "And who gave you the right to decide for me anyway? What if I refuse to go with you?"

He may have triggered her anger by acting similarly to her parents, pushing away her ability to choose. "It is rationally the best choice right now," he declared calmly.

Tessa grumbled under her breath but he could not hear what she said.

Kieran wasn't used to dealing with people, no less women, on a deeper emotional level. He did well with it socially, but only to a point. "Listen, I... I don't know what to say, but I need you with me to get to the bottom of this case and do my job," he said, bordering on both frustrated and anxious, "and staying with me is the best option you have for staying safe."

Tessa did not respond or acknowledge his words.

"So. You can keep running from these guys forever," he narrowed his golden eyes at her, "or we can bring them down together. You tell me what the best choice is, Tessa."

Tessa sighed irritably, but he could sense that she was now seeing his point and understood him. "Fine," she said, lifting her head to look directly at the minty bounty hunter, "I'll stay with you. If you insist. I wash my hands of your blood if something happens to you; there's only so much I can do to save idiots."

The bounty hunter cracked a small, half-smile on his muzzle; he could tell Tessa was reacting this way out of concern for him. They may not have known each other long, but it was clear that she had a big heart.

The blue fox saw his expression and blushed a little, then took a sip of her coffee. "Just... I don't know you, so please don't be a creep," she said in a low voice, stirring.

"You have my word, miss," he responded warmly. "Let's enjoy the coffee and treats. Then we'll go somewhere safe."

It was highly likely that he was already a target anyway, so getting involved with Tessa would not hurt him further.

Taking a bite of his vanilla cream donut, he tasted the rich flavors coating his tongue. "Oh..! This tastes like Heaven!" he exclaimed, adding flair to his statement by 'talking' with his hand-paws.

Tessa still looked apprehensive but gave a subtle smile. "Yea. This place has great donuts. Have you tried any of their cakes yet?"

"No," he perked up his ears curiously.

"What is your favorite flavor of dessert, then?"

"Uh... apples?"

"They have apple cakes. Come on, let's go order, I'll pay."

CHAPTER SIX

BLANKET OF DARKNESS

Beneath the cloak of night, Kieran and Tessa silently threaded their way through the labyrinthine, cobblestone streets of Dawnbreak. The moon, a pale lantern in the sky, cast fleeting shadows as they moved toward the city's outskirts.

Tessa, concealed in a light brown hooded cloak that Isabella had given her just before they departed, walked beside Kieran with a grace born of both caution and curiosity. The minty fox had also grabbed all of his supplies and weapons, his backpack fastened over his shoulders as well as his bow.

Perseus nestled at the nape of her neck in the hood, an easily concealed little dragon. He remained silent, knowing full well that stealth was necessary at that moment. A smart dragon indeed!

The city, in the shroud of night, wore a different face — a tapestry of muted colors and dimly candlelit windows. As they reached the city's edge, Kieran cast a glance back at the sleeping silhouette of the quaint settlement. The city's secrets whispered in the rustle of midnight winds seemed to fade into the backdrop.

Kieran, attuned to the ebb and flow of the night, led Tessa with the assurance of one who navigates the witching hour. Their destination lay beyond the city's embrace, where the rocky outcroppings awaited, promising a temporary refuge beneath the stars.

The journey, marked by the rhythmic cadence of footsteps, carried the weight of unspoken questions. Surely, though, they'd have plenty of time to talk alone and not be monitored by anyone when they properly made camp outside the walls.

In the quiet passage from city to wilderness, Tessa's green eyes, covered beneath the clothing she wore, observed the nocturnal world with a blend of doubt and inquisitiveness.

As they neared a narrow alleyway, a tense dialogue reached Kieran's sharp ears. He held up a paw, signaling Tessa to pause, and soundlessly moved forward, keeping out of anyone's eyesight as best as he could.

Tessa got on her hands and knees behind some wood logs, obeying Kieran's guidance.

The brave minty fox crouched and sneaked along, until ahead of him was where one could turn a corner. He made his way slowly, careful not to let even the claws on his feet-paws drag on the stone below. Each footstep was placed with the utmost care and attention.

He came upon the corner, where he looked through the cracks of a wooden crate. From the concealment of the dark crate, Kieran's ears twitched as he discerned the murmur of voices.

In the dimly lit space, he could see a disquieting scene unfolding — a lone guard, clad in the familiar armor of Dawnbreak's guard force, surrounded by fellow sentinels. The tension in the air was palpable, that much was easy to tell on the spot.

'But... why? What's going on?' he wondered.

"Keep your muzzle shut, Hans," one of the guards sneered, a brown fox with amber eyes, his voice dripping with menace. "You didn't see anything, got it? If you breathe a word about what happened tonight, you'll wish you never wore that armor."

Hans, a white fox, cornered against the alley's cold stone walls, wore a conflicted expression. The badge on his chest gleamed weakly in the scant light.

"I can't lie about this, Voss," Hans replied, a glimmer of defiance in his red eyes. "Malachai's escape will have consequences. I won't be part of a cover-up."

The tension escalated, long shadow figures dancing on the brick walls that enclosed them as the guards closed in, their voices a threatening crescendo. Kieran listened intently, his golden eyes narrowed with concern. Was he about to witness something terrible?

"Besides," Hans said bravely, though trembling was evident in both his body and voice, "I know you'll take my life tonight anyway."

"For the last time, Hans," Voss growled irritably, his patience worn thin. "Swear on your life, you won't utter a word about what transpired. We have our reasons, and you don't want to find out what happens if you defy us."

The other guards with Voss snarled, their white fangs flashing here and there, hands on their swords, ready to draw at a moment's notice, hands quivering with clear excitement at the thought of some action. Low guttural growls reverberated from their throats.

Hans, though surrounded, held onto his principles like a flickering flame against the encroaching shadows. "I won't betray my duty. Dawnbreak deserves better than a guard who compromises its safety for the sake of his own life."

Voss exchanged a glance with his accomplices, and an unspoken agreement was reached. In the gloomy alley, the betrayal played out like a tragic theater, and Kieran, hidden from view, felt the gravity of the situation.

The guards lunged at Hans, their blows landing with brutal precision.

Just like that, Hans' white coat was stained crimson red with his blood. Once he was on the ground, Voss signaled for his lackeys to stay put and moved closer to Hans, his blade drawn.

"Too bad," he said, chillingly calm, "you were a great man. You would have been invaluable to us."

Hans looked up with terror in his eyes, breathing fast and heavy, knowing his time was coming any second. He trembled as if bitten with winter's frost. With that, Voss swung his sword and slashed open the throat of the poor white fox.

His cries of pain mingled with the sound of gurgling his blood echoed in the confined space. The silver badge that once symbolized honor now gleamed with bitter sorrow as Hans crumpled to the stone-cold ground, his life extinguished.

Blood that appeared black in the lack of light ebbed from his body, thickening in his fur, filling his mouth, and drenching his fangs. His red eyes dimmed as his life force faded, remaining blankly open.

Kieran felt a surge of anger and sorrow. Hans' sacrifice for truth was met with a savage response, a stark reminder of the ruthless undercurrents that pulsed beneath the veneer of order in Dawnbreak. As the lifeblood of the slain guard stained the cobblestones, Kieran clutched his dagger, torn between a desire for justice and the necessity to keep moving for the sake of his quest.

As much as it angered him to let these evil pieces of horse dung go without punishment, he knew it was the right choice; he was outnumbered and was responsible for Tessa's safety. Before he was seen, he backed away from the scene, and when out of earshot he burst away at high speed toward where his temporary companion was hidden among the lumber.

Kieran gripped Tessa's arm, pulling her away from the gruesome place; she remained quiet, knowing better than to give away their position, but he could tell that she was very afraid. The scent of the murder lingered in the air, metallic and sodden.

They moved swiftly through the outskirts, away from the city's heart where corruption festered like a wound. The minty blue fox's mind was a tempest of conflicting emotions, a tsunami of unanswered questions.

The bounty hunter and the starry girl made their way hurriedly out of the city.

As they reached a rocky sanctuary on the plains, Kieran couldn't shake the image of Hans' lifeless eyes from his mind. Once he felt they were far enough into the plains to not be watched or overheard by any sapient threat, he turned to Tessa, his voice carrying the weight of their grim reality.

"The guards of Dawnbreak are corrupt. They just killed their own for finding out the truth, that they let Malachai escape," he said with heaviness.

Tessa covered her mouth in shock, very upset by this news. "What do we do now?" she asked, her voice steady but with an underlying tremor.

Kieran put his hand on her shoulder, attempting to give the star fox comfort. "Stay out here for a bit, then come up with a plan going forward."

Tessa nodded, loosening up a bit, clearly feeling at least somewhat safe with the minty fox around to guard her. "I'll follow your lead... but, please, let's hurry up and get to a hiding place, I hate being out in the open when such threats are around."

Kieran took her hand and led her through the dewy plains grass toward the dark gray rocky terrain on the horizon. There they'd make a home, for now, in a place that was unlikely to be sought out by undesirables.

Kieran's knowledge of the natural world and survival skills drove them to a secluded spot, nestled amidst the craggy formations.

It would provide enough cover to keep them both hidden, but it also would shelter them from the elements. The rocks were a shade of blue-gray under the black sky, its texture, and details, muted in the cover of night.

Kieran and Tessa set to work under the big outcropping, efficiently assembling his tent; they didn't need it, but comfort was well appreciated where possible. It would provide them with an additional layer of privacy, too, which Kieran assumed was important to Tessa as a woman...

especially one staying with a man she was not romantically involved with at all.

The ground was a mix of rock and dirt, so they chose a spot with the most dirt to put up the tent.

Kieran reached into his bag and pulled out a blanket, handing it to the blue star fox. "Here. Sleep inside."

Tessa took it, feeling its softness. She looked at him gratefully. "Thanks. You really are a gentleman."

To be honest, Kieran hadn't spent much time around women in his life. He was completely unused to this whole "gentleman" thing, but he was acting on instinct alone. A woman needed a comfy place to stay, and protection by a strong man... any man, it didn't matter.

"I try," he said, facing away, busying himself with the set up of his own bed outside the tent.

Kieran didn't know if he was attracted to her particularly, or if he was simply just feeling a sense of primal duty which was leading him to feel attracted solely because she was a female. He hadn't seen or interacted with a girl in months, at least, before arriving in the Highland Plains city of Dawnbreak.

This was natural for a guy, either way, but he chose to ignore it. The minty fox had to keep this professional, for one, and as nice as mating would be after the stress he'd gone through the past couple of days Tessa was not the right choice... not after what she had just experienced, and certainly not after what she'd said in the coffee shop.

She did not fully trust him, which was completely understandable, so he needed to show her he was a good man.

Putting those thoughts out of his mind, he finished setting up his bed on the soft soil on raised ground. He'd have a blanket to help keep in the heat, as well as a good vantage point to keep watch over the camp.

Once everything was arranged, Kieran and Tessa sat close together, the glow of a small fire casting wavy shadows on the huge stone crags. The crackle of flames and the distant hum of nocturnal creatures filled the air. The howling of a far-away wolf pack danced on the hills and through the nooks and crannies of the cliffs. Perseus played with the campfire, which was made of scattered sticks and logs they'd gathered. Kieran looked at Tessa beside him, a poignancy in his golden eyes. "We're safe here for a while, but we need to talk about what comes next."

Tessa appeared downtrodden. "You don't have to help them, you know."

The minty fox perked up his ears and looked at her with light confusion. "What do you mean?"

"You can just leave this place anytime. Why do you want to endanger yourself for others?" Her words carried a weight of uncertainty and fear.

Kieran raised a brow and stared at her silently for a moment. "This is my job." He replied, keeping his response concise, though the complexity of his motivations remained untold.

The blue fox said no more, and rested her head on her knees with her arms wrapped around her face, watching the flames crackle and the smoke rise.

A cold wind coursed through their shelter from outside, giving them both a shiver. Kieran's fur stood on end from the wind, his ears whipping around. "I know you're scared. That is normal for a female. I'm feeling it too, but we can overcome it."

Tessa growled in frustration, her green eyes burning with defiance. "I am not afraid!"

'What is her problem?' Kieran wondered, his fur ruffling in the cold wind. Despite the mild irritation, he spoke with a measured calmness. "There's nothing wrong with being afraid, Tessa."

"You said it's just because I'm a woman," she retorted, ears flattened.

"I said I was fearful too," Kieran reiterated, his voice steady.

He couldn't quite fathom the source of her irritation, but a subtle tension remained. Kieran, choosing his words carefully, continued, "But we need to be on the same page. I can't do this alone, and neither can you. We're safer together, and besides, we have a common goal – to expose the corruption in Dawnbreak and bring justice to those who deserve it."

"That's exactly what I don't understand about you, though," Tessa burned, throwing her hand-paws up in the air, "Why aren't you running? What compels you to not just escape and find another, easier case someplace else?"

Kieran was about to respond, but stopped himself; he knew the answer, but it involved a subject matter that he usually was not comfortable talking about. He wanted to bring terrible people to justice so they would not hurt anyone else, and this was inspired by his history.

Perseus lashed his tail and ogled Kieran cautiously, ready to attack if need be. He did not know if his partner was in danger or not, he just knew she was not feeling good and that these feelings seemed to be caused by the bounty hunter.

"It's just not what a man does," he stated confidently. "We don't run."

This seemed to upset Tessa further. She was about to argue but stopped herself when she saw

Kieran's solemn expression. After a few seconds, she let out a defeated sigh and said, "Alright."

Kieran knew she had some feelings she was not admitting to him, though he could not begin to understand what they were. He reasoned that it wasn't worth probing, since it wasn't important comparatively to the issue at hand.

The minty-furred fox leaned in, his voice low. "I have contacts, people who might help us. But first, we need to uncover the full extent of this corruption. I have a few ideas, but it's going to be dangerous."

Tessa lightened up a bit as if forgetting the previous exchange between them. "How are you going to do it?" she inquired, curiously.

Kieran took a deep breath through his nostrils and stared out into the moonlit landscape. "I'm going to have to think about that."

CHAPTER SEVEN

BOUNTY HUNTER'S STRATEGY

The cobbled streets of Dawnbreak were eerily silent, a stark contrast to the usual hustle and bustle. Shadows, thick and menacing, clung to the sides of buildings like malevolent spirits. The air, heavy with foreboding, pressed down on him as he moved through the darkened city.

The stones beneath his paws transformed into pools of inky blackness, each step leaving boisterous ripples. A distant wail echoed, chilling Kieran to his core. Terror gripped his being, against his will. As he turned toward the sound, he saw the dim outline of what appeared to be Hans standing in the center of town.

The air itself seemed to thicken, making it hard to breathe.

In a macabre dance, the corrupt guards materialized around Hans. Their eyes glowed red with malevolence, a sickly light that cast grotesque black wisps across their faces. Voss, the orchestrator of this twisted episode, emerged from the mass pool of ink, his silhouette imposing and malice.

Kieran gasped for air, finding less and less oxygen. His mind panicked; in desperation, he used every bit of strength he had to draw in as much air as he could.

The shadows came alive, wrapping around Hans like serpents, constricting tighter with each passing moment. Reality itself broke as the white fox glitched and broke apart, letting out a deafening scream that shook the world.

A dark, viscous substance oozed from the ground, staining everything in its path. A scent of metallic assaulted his nose, and it was so strong that tears formed in his eyes.

The mint-furred fox was rooted to the spot, helpless against the nightmarish imagery unfolding before him. The inky pools turned to blood, which ever so violently coursed at his feet-paws.

With Hans' existence eradicated, Voss and his lackeys turned their attention toward the bounty hunter. Their eyes were uncannily large and completely circular. They menacingly gazed at him, cracking a predatory grin that showed off their razor-sharp fangs. Kieran's heart pounded in fear as he watched them slowly make their way toward him, a static noise growing louder and louder until it was ear-piercing.

While feelings of despair and imminent death grew within him, Kieran's resolve did too. He felt anger rising in his heart, as he did when in any combat scenario. The golden-eyed fox bared his teeth against fate, a flame alive in his soul that craved the life force of his enemies. It would not stop until it was thoroughly satisfied, not until it had drunk as many chalices of it as it so desired.

The shades of the corrupt guards lunged at him with a ghastly shriek, and in a flash had him held down, face and muzzle plunged forcefully into the murky liquid beneath. All power was stripped from him, and no amount of effort yielded any kind of headway; he could not for the life of him free himself. Eventually, running out of air, he inhaled the river of blood.

Then, with a gasp, Kieran woke and shot up to a sitting position.

His chest heaved deeply, adrenaline pumping in his veins. It took a few moments for it to kick in for the stressed fox that the struggle he'd just experienced was all in his head, but soon the sweetest sensation of relief flooded over him, and his heart calmed down to a rest.

The first rays of the dawn's pale light trickled into the rocky shelter, and a gentle, warm breeze brushed against Kieran's drowsy face and toned chest. Pushing himself to his feet, Kieran shook off the remnants of the dream, his golden eyes scanning the tranquil surroundings. The rocks, bathed in the soft hues of the morning sun, stood as silent witnesses to the turmoil within him.

The death of Hans had been haunting to him; sure, the minty fox had seen plenty of violence and killing, even done it himself at times, but it was the context here that disturbed him so much. If it had just been the usual killing to escape capture or to steal goods like he was used to with the criminals he dealt with, he would be fine because he was desensitized to it; but this was something different, something far sinister than he had ever known.

'I've never hunted the authorities before,' he thought to himself as he made his way to the edge of the shelter, inches from the outside grass, *'and*

there's so many of them; there's no telling how many are corrupt or not.'

Kieran stood on a rock face, overlooking the shimmering, contrasty landscape. This was his favorite hour of day and was when he'd usually relax and draw in his art journal before taking on the new sun, but this time it felt like the weight of the world was on his shoulders. To be fair, it wasn't the first bout of such a thing in his life.

He sat down and exhaled slowly. *'I'll need to think of something... a plan. I have to keep Tessa safe, and out of the wrong hand. I need to find a way to deal with the corruption.'*

For a good, long while he sat in contemplation, the jagged rocks beneath him providing an uneven seat. Soon enough, he came up with some ideas to move forward with his mission. The crux of it lay in seeking help, and he knew exactly the ally he needed – his best friend, Liam O'Brien.

Now all he had to do was inform Tessa about it, so the minty-furred fox looked around and over at the tent she was sleeping in. Perseus, the vigilant dragon, curled up at the entrance, guarding with profound loyalty as per usual, his fiery scales gleaming in the early light.

Now and again, his forked tongue would drawl out on the ground.

Kieran approached the tent, his movements gentle as he peered in, opened the flaps, and reached in to wake Tessa.

He crouched beside her, shaking her shoulder. Perseus eyed him watchfully once again but remained still. "Tessa," he called softly, repeating it until he saw the stirrings of wakefulness in her green eyes.

She emerged from the realm of dreams, confusion painted her features. "What's going on?" she asked, a trace of sleepiness still in her voice.

Kieran sighed, his breath visible in the cool morning air. "I have a plan. This mission is bigger than I thought. I have a friend, Liam O'Brien. He's trustworthy, and he can help us root out the corruption in Dawnbreak."

Tessa blinked.

Kieran tilted his head. "Did you get that?"

Tessa snuggled into her pillow, closing her eyes. "It's too early in the morning for this. Let me sleep more."

Kieran huffed in amusement and rolled his eyes. 'Girls.'

"You'll need to wakey-wakey, sweetheart. We're in a very serious situation, there's no time to waste lazing about," he instructed emphatically.

Tessa groaned, burying her face deeper into the pillow. "I hate mornings."

Kieran chuckled, his eyes glinting with determination. "Mornings hate corrupt officials even more. Come on, Tessa, you're stronger than you think. We've got work to do."

With a reluctant sigh, Tessa finally opened her eyes, meeting Kieran's gaze. "Fine."

Kieran grinned, pleased that she was coming around. "Trust me. Liam is the key to unraveling this mess. Now, let's get some breakfast, and I'll fill you in on the plan. We have a long day ahead, and we need to be prepared."

A moment of silence followed, the blue star fox giving Kieran a serious glare. "Can I have some privacy?" she asked.

Kieran flattened his ears, a little confused at first but then he got it and pulled out of the tent. "Oh, right, yes."

He surely was not used to inhabiting the same space as a woman.

Once both of them were ready to head out to find food, Kieran led them deeper into the cliffs. He would have preferred if Perseus had stayed behind to keep watch over their hideout, but there was no way the dragon would have allowed Tessa out of his sight.

He scanned the ground and walls for any indication of a burrow or nest. He was a skilled hunter, of course, having to feed himself during travel in the unoccupied wilderness all these years.

He'd taken down great beasts such as deer and wolves before, as well as the smaller critters like squirrels and raccoons; they'd all been a lovely feast.

The minty fox sure did love his meaty meals, as well as the coats and bones of the animals he killed; it provided a way to make extra gold, and ways to keep warm without having to go out and survey markets for a good blanket.

Oh yes, Kieran was good at tanning pelts, too! He'd learned a lot from his mentor in his teenage years. Garrick Ironheart was his name, a spunky old fox, beaten in appearance but not lacking in spirit within at all.

It had been a long time since he'd seen Garrick; perhaps one day soon the bounty hunter would set off on a journey to visit the old-timer. *'After I deal with Dawnbreak,'* Kieran decided, gazing at the cloudy, blue sky for a moment.

With Garrick Ironheart's teachings echoing in his mind, he moved with a predatory grace, every step deliberate and silent. Beside him, Tessa observed, her eyes wide with a mix of curiosity and trepidation.

The scent of wild herbs mingled with the earthy aroma of the cliffs. Kieran spotted a small group of rabbits nibbling on sparse grass, unaware of the duo closing in.

He signaled for Tessa to stay put, his fingers lightly touching her back before he melted into the natural surroundings.

The starry fox did as she was told, hiding behind a big dead tree that lay sprawled on the ground among rocks.

His bow, crafted with care and precision, was drawn silently. The minty-furred fox moved with the fluidity of a snake, blending into the crags. His breath slowed as he aimed for the largest rabbit in the group. The arrow released with a soft whisper, swiftly finding its mark.

The unfortunate prey fell with minimal resistance, letting out a curt squeak. Kieran approached it with a calculated calmness. He dispatched it swiftly, Garrick's lessons evident in every efficient movement. The task was routine, a dance of survival that spoke to the primal instincts ingrained in both fox and rabbit.

Returning to Tessa, Kieran offered a small, reassuring smile. The lifeless rabbit, now slung over his shoulder. "Let's head back and clean the carcass," he explained, breaking the tension in the air.

"Clean it?" She raised a brow curiously.

"That means to prepare it for cooking," he explained enthusiastically. Passing by her, he let out a barely audible giggle, leading them back to camp; the minty fox was beginning to remind himself of his mentor Ironheart, passing on what he had learned from him to someone else.

As the fire crackled, Kieran expertly skewered the rabbit on a makeshift spit. The aroma of roasting meat filled the air, intertwining with the natural scents around them.

Tessa watched the flames dance, her face reflecting a mix of hunger and anticipation. The pair sat close, and Kieran rotated the spit, ensuring an even cook, the sizzling sound harmonizing with the nocturnal chorus of distant creatures.

"Ugh, it smells so good!" Tessa beamed with anticipation.

Kieran's mouth watered. He was so hungry!

The cooked rabbit, now a tantalizing golden brown, was presented with a certain pride. Kieran carved it with one of his sharp blades, the succulent meat revealing itself beneath the crispy exterior. He handed a portion to Tessa, the heat and steam still rising from the savory meal.

They ate their share. The minty fox occasionally stole glances at Tessa, gauging her reaction to the breakfast he'd prepared.

Tessa savored a bite of the rabbit, and she lit up with appreciation. "Kieran, this is amazing. Seriously, you're like a gourmet chef in the wild or something."

Kieran chuckled, a hint of pride in his golden eyes. "I'm glad you like it. Survival skills include knowing how to make a good meal out of whatever you've got."

She nodded, taking another bite. "Well, you've definitely got the knack for it. I appreciate it, especially after how I acted last night. I shouldn't have... been so rude."

Kieran glanced at her, his expression softened. "No worries. We've both got a lot on our plates, metaphorically and literally. Apology accepted."

Tessa smiled, a genuine warmth in her eyes. "Thanks. I know you're just trying to help."

They continued to eat in companionable silence. The morning sun had fully risen, and its affable glow mingled with the comforting heat of the fire. It felt like a brand new day because it truly was; a fresh start amidst the challenges they faced.

Kieran, holding a skewer with a piece of rabbit, turned to the girl. "Tessa, I've decided; we can't linger in Dawnbreak any longer," he began, his voice low but resolute. "We need to slip away and head east into the Emberlands. That's where my contact, Liam O'Brien, is located. He can help us with our endeavor."

Tessa, curious and a little bit concerned, listened intently. She took a bite of food, savoring the flavors, before responding. "But... it'll take us weeks to get there."

Kieran shook his head, smiling giddily, proud of himself for the idea he'd concocted. "Nope. I have a plan." The flames crackled over his voice. "It's best if no one sees you, so we can't make a scene by getting horses, nor can we take a carriage there, but what we can do is hitch a ride on the Veridis Express."

Tessa raised her brows, impressed with the genius of his idea, as well as excited for the coming adventure. "Oh? That's not bad, actually," she commented, grinning as she looked to the side. As

Tessa processed the audacious plan, a spark of excitement lit up in her eyes, and she looked back at the bounty hunter. "So, you're going to get us on a moving train? Without anyone noticing?"

"Exactly! It's our ticket out of here. We sneak on board in an empty train car and let it whisk us away to the Emberlands. It's faster and safer than trudging through the wilderness on foot," Kieran winked, his confidence unwavering. "I've done crazier things, trust me. With the hustle and bustle of people boarding and disembarking, we'll blend right in. It's the perfect way to slip away unnoticed."

Tessa chuckled, impressed by Kieran's audacity. "Alright, Kieran, I'm in."

Perseus snorted a cloud of fiery sparks as if offering his somewhat reluctant praise.

"Will we do this today?" she asked. Kieran dipped his head, scratching behind his ears. "Yes. The longer we stay, the greater the risk. We can't do this on our own; the corruption is much bigger than we are. We need to move discreetly, to avoid drawing attention."

Tessa's gaze depressed downward, a little sad. "What about Malachai?"

The minty fox huffed, displeased to even hear the name, and reached for a steel-tipped arrow from his quiver. He held it out before his female companion. "If he shows his ugly face, I'll put one of these between his eyes," he promised.

From what he could tell, his words seemed to make her feel more comforted about going forward.

After they had finished their welcome meal and were satisfied, full of energy to face what lay ahead of them, they packed up everything they had and set off to catch the steam train. Tessa secured her hooded cloak, concealing her identity as Perseus curled around her neck, hidden inside. Kieran, his movements fluid and purposeful, checked the supplies, making sure everything was stowed away securely. He slung his bow over his shoulder and adjusted the straps of his leather outfit. The sun hung high in the sky, bathing the city in warm golds and reds, sending light bouncing everywhere.

Dawnbreak truly was a magnificent place. If Kieran did not know any better, he'd assume it was safe, too.

The pair, armed with determination and a shared goal, moved with stealth toward the tracks. As they navigated the crowds, Kieran glanced at Tessa, catching the glint of excitement in her shadowed jade eyes.

"We need to make like swift foxes now. The train won't wait for us," Kieran murmured, his voice low in the afternoon heat. A cool summer breeze fanned through their pelts.

As they made their way through the train station, the distant sound of a steam engine whistle reached their ears. The Veridis Express was preparing to depart, dark plumes of thick, chewy smoke billowing upward into the light cornflower blue sky. Kieran quickened his pace, leading the way with certitude.

Tessa followed suit, making very sure to stay close to his side; she did not want to lag, or even worse, get left behind and cause a rift in their plan.

Upon reaching the entrance to the platform they saw the train, its sleek charcoal gray form shrouded in hot, swelling steam, ready to embark on its few-day-long trek to the foreign nation in the east. The polished, cherry-wood plank platform was alive with activity as passengers bustled about, packed in together, their attention focused on boarding and finding their seats.

Kieran surveyed the scene, his mind calculating the best approach. It was not the passenger cars that he wanted, but the storage cars; he knew the Veridis Express line of transport stored food and other useful supplies in the back of their trains, and these cars usually had plenty of room to stowaway, far from any peaking eyes for the majority of the duration of the journey.

The minty fox moved ahead and waited close to the tracks as everyone around him boarded until the group of people thinned and the last passenger section pulled up; this meant that they could hop into the storage expeditiously, without drawing notice.

Like a creature latent in the foliage, one with its surroundings, the bounty hunter did what he did best; he hopped onto the train and disappeared into the blackness of the car, the starry blue fox girl with, in a matter of a single second. There was a low chance that anyone had noticed, and if they had then they'd likely think it was their imagination.

The rhythmic clatter of the train's wheels echoed through the metal confines, creating a soothing symphony of motion. The air was heavy with the scent of oil and machinery, an olfactory testament to the relentless pilgrimage ahead.

The storage compartment, though dimly lit from outside, offered a haven of respite. Boxes and crates were neatly stacked, their contents secured. Kieran motioned for Tessa to find a quiet corner to sit and relax in with her dragon guardian, as the train's steady acceleration sent a subtle vibration through the floor.

Tessa settled against a stack of crates, her eyes reflecting a blend of fatigue and exhilaration. The blue fox took a deep breath, attempting to steady her racing heart. Perseus curled around her but kept his guard up, sniffing the air. He remained tense.

"Good riddance to this place," Tessa giggled happily, clearly feeling a huge weight off her shoulders. "It'll be nice to see new places, far away from the people who are hunting me."

Kieran, ever vigilant, scanned the surroundings before joining his travel partner. He sank onto a pile of sacks, his minty fur absorbing the gentle hum of the train's movement, shaking now and again.

The measured click-clack of the wheels on the tracks became a lullaby, soothing the edges of their nerves.

Kieran and Tessa exchanged glances, a silent acknowledgment of the difficult circumstance that they had overcome together, and of the force propelling them into the unknown territory far away. The veracious wheels of the Veridis Express spun tales of new horizons and undreamed dangers.

The landscape outside blurred into streaks of green and gold, a visual testament to the alacrity of their departure. The occasional jolt and sway became a natural cadence, lulling them into a transient reprieve.

The whistle of the wind went on and on, creating a relaxing atmosphere. As the Express gathered speed, hurtling through the landscape, getting further and further from the dense city, Tessa and Kieran huddled near each other attempting to fall asleep for a nap.

It was comfortable enough with there being hay scattered about.

However, Kieran, ever vigilant, surveyed the surroundings with the instinctual caution of a seasoned bounty hunter.

The open door framed a rapidly changing land, a blur of hills and wildflower-painted fields that made a picturesque scene outside.

CHAPTER EIGHT

THE RUBY DAGGERS

The clinking of metal against metal caught his attention, waking him from his light sleep. Kieran's ears pricked up, and he turned his gaze upward. To his astonishment, a figure detached itself from the train's roof, landing with an eerie grace in the storage car. The newcomer wore an ensemble of black leather, the muted tones blending seamlessly with the dark surroundings. His fur, reminiscent of a black wolf, was a mixture of cool brown shades, darker cool brown arms and legs, and a similarly darker brown covering his face.

The new male stood poised like a coiled serpent ready to strike. His presence emanated an unsettling feel, enhanced by the unnerving giggles that rumbled within his concealed features. A red bandanna wrapped around his muzzle and neck, an ominous accent that spoke volumes about his nefarious intent.

Kieran's senses flared, adrenaline coursing through his veins, as he instinctively reached for his weapons.

Tessa, initially oblivious to the looming threat, felt the shift in the atmosphere and woke up immediately. She saw the intruder, and gasped as she looked at Kieran terrified, who wore an expression of focused intensity. The minty-furred bounty hunter motioned for her to stay low and silent, his eyes never leaving the ominous figure now standing before them.

In a swift, protective motion, Kieran stepped in front of Tessa, shielding her with his lithe frame. His stare bore into the mysterious intruder, a wordless declaration that he would not let any harm befall the blue-furred fox under his watch. His fists clenched onto his daggers, his brows furrowed, and he assumed a defensive stance.

Kieran would have thought it'd be Malachai hitching a ride and then finding them here, but... no, it was not. "We don't want any trouble," he grumbled loud enough for the stranger to hear, and firmly. "You can stay here with us as long as you don't do anything suspicious."

Maybe he'd had the same idea they did, in which case Kieran was happy to offer the benefit of a doubt.

The brown fox emitted a low growl that reverberated through the confined space. His lips curled into a sinister snarl, revealing gleaming fangs. The eerie giggles that sounded from within his obscured features added a chilling layer to the encounter. "You're in my way," the male fox hissed, the words laden with threat. The red bandanna shifted slightly as he spoke, a sinister dance against the muted backdrop of his dark fur.

Kieran, sensing the malevolent intent radiating from the intruder, decided that a direct confrontation was necessary. He swiftly unsheathed his two gleaming, silver daggers, the blades catching the dim light of the storage car.

Tessa, crouched behind him, watched with fear and trust as her protector prepared for the impending clash.

The stranger snarled and charged at Kieran, eyes alight with rage, swinging his pair of wickedly sharp daggers like a wild animal. His daggers were steel with the inner bits of the blade made of shining red ruby. It was dramatically serrated, having not just teeth but fangs to gash and tear through flesh.

Kieran lunged forward, aiming to disarm the brown fox and neutralize the threat. Blade hit blade with a schick noise, and many clangs. The male physique of both foxes aided them greatly in holding each other back, hopping away and lunging again; they did this a few times, Kieran making sure to stay in front of Tessa, preventing all access to her.

His movements were precise and calculated, his golden eyes focused on anticipating every strike. The intruder, however, moved with a feral agility, dodging and parrying Kieran's attacks with unsettling grace. The lethal dance continued, each combatant attempting to gain the upper hand. Tessa, keenly aware of the danger, remained huddled, ready to follow Kieran's lead if she needed to.

Exploiting a momentary lapse in Kieran's defense, the stranger disarmed him with a swift, well-placed strike. The minty fox's daggers clattered to the floor, and in a flash he found himself there too, pinned on his back. Kieran looked up at the victor, grimacing, feeling fear on the inside but unwilling to show it. Tessa's jade eyes widened, a gasp escaping her as the situation took a dire turn. Perseus watched closely, never taking his piercing gaze off his friend's protector.

"I would love nothing more than to shed a little blood right now," said the brown fox, licking his maw then giggling with an edge of unhinged.

Victorious in this skirmish, the intruder stood over Kieran, his ruby-fanged daggers poised for a finishing blow, pointed rigidly down at him. The eerie giggles persisted, filling the air with a chilling malevolence. It was clear this male was insane to some degree. "What do you want, madman?" Kieran hissed through clenched teeth.

The intruder grinned as he spoke in a low whisper. "Give me the girl, and you can go free," he spat, then burst into laughter. "Free! Like the crazy dog you are! Oh, my goodness, yes mister Riven here will let you go, yes he will."

'*No. Absolutely not,*' Kieran thought. He'd faced the threat of death many times head on, and he'd learned not to waver in the moment. He had decided long ago to stick with his convictions and not falter. The minty bounty hunter furrowed his brows at the fox, whom he supposed was named Riven based on what he said, and wondered how he could proceed from here.

Kieran looked over at Perseus. '*Come on... come on, you need to help us. Don't you care about Tessa?*' he thought, hoping the dragon would respond to his pleading eyes.

Kieran turned back to Riven and muttered, "You think I'd give up that easily?" Before Riven could react, Kieran unleashed a rapid series of movements, a well-practiced maneuver he had learned from his mentor, Garrick Ironheart. He twisted his legs around Riven's and knocked his off balance, the brown fox crashing to the ground under the force. The minty bounty hunter managed to disarm one of the daggers, sending it clattering across the floor.

Riven roared and lunged at Kieran, fangs ready to sink into him. However, just before the dreadful attacker could deliver a bite, a sudden blur of scales and fire burst onto the scene. Perseus had finally chosen to join the fight.

Perseus' colossal form loomed over Riven, a mountainous barrier of orange, black and white scales that seemed impervious to the struggles of the captive beneath. The air resonated with the growls and roars, a symphony of fury and pain as the dragon unleashed his wrath upon the intruder.

Riven's futile attempts to free himself were met with the unyielding strength of Perseus, who retaliated with a menacing snarl and the sharp graze of his jet black claws.

Perseus had transformed into his bigger form, the one Kieran had seen the other night. Fire boiled in his mouth, which hung slightly open. Tessa stared at the scene in both relief and a bit of fear.

Kieran got up quickly and attempted to get Perseus' attention. "Hey, hey..." Kieran began, his voice a calming force in the chaos. As Perseus acknowledged him with a glance, Kieran continued, "Let me have him. I'll tie him up. We can ask him a few questions."

With a practiced efficiency, Kieran seized nearby rope, quickly restraining Riven's hands and feet. Perseus maintained his vigil, ensuring the captive remained subdued, the fiery glow in his eyes betraying a deep-seated anger. The brown fox could do nothing to fight them off, and was then securely bound and tethered to a hefty wooden crate; he found himself at the mercy of his captors.

As the tension eased, Kieran exhaled a heavy sigh, the weight of the encounter lifting from his shoulders. Perseus, still in his formidable form, exuded a silent readiness, his eyes fixed on Riven with a seething animosity, his black mane flowing in the train car's cross breeze.

Tessa, her ears down-turned, moved closer to Kieran, her expression a mixture of fear and gratitude. The silence between them spoke volumes, a shared acknowledgment of the relentless dangers they faced.

Perseus stood like a royal beast, his imposing form dominating the limited space. He remained in his greater form, the train car's cross breeze playing with the strands of his fiery-colored mane, which did not fit around his neck like a lion but rather it sat on top of his body from forehead to tail tip like a horse's mane.

His red eyes burned with hatred for the attacker, and Kieran could tell that he wanted to get his claws on him far more than he'd allowed himself to. Perseus' huge black horns pointed backward, and sat majestically.

The swaying of the tracks did nothing to disturb Perseus from his poise; he remained vigilant, eyes locked on Riven's position.

As Tessa nestled closer, she said nothing, and a question echoed in Kieran's mind — how long had she been living under the shadows of relentless pursuit? The minty fox, usually adept at deciphering the complexities of the world, found himself unable to fully grasp the depths of her past. Yet, he could sense the resilience within her, the unyielding spirit that had carried her through unknown perils.

'Poor girl,' he sympathized.

Kieran could only imagine what she'd been through before meeting him. She'd managed to stay safe with her dragon actively defending her for this long, but it was becoming apparent that these attacks were getting stronger for her.

A guttural growl tore through the air, dragging Kieran's attention away from the subtle interplay of shadows within the train car. The growly voice, emanating from Riven, pierced through the silence like a discordant note in a symphony of quiet contemplation.

"I need Tessa. To make this world better," Riven declared, his words laced with an unsettling conviction that echoed against the metal walls.

The minty fox's golden eyes narrowed as he turned to face the source of the ominous statement. His gaze bore into Riven, a mixture of disdain and frustration etched across his features. "You asshole," Kieran retorted sharply, the tension in his voice cutting through the confined space.

"Whoever you're associated with needs to stop hunting her. You people just come in, blades out, hoping to kill your way to whatever... goals you have."

Riven's response was a disdainful scrunch of his nose, a feral snarl unveiling the sharp edges of his teeth. The red bandanna around his neck seemed to tighten with the menace in the air. "Our goal is freedom and kindness for all," he declared.

Kieran's skepticism lingered in the air like a charged static, his gaze unyielding. The dissonance between Riven's professed ideals and the violence he embodied hung palpably in the confined space of the train car, leaving an unsettling tension that begged for resolution.

A wry smirk played upon Kieran's minty muzzle as he responded to Riven's lofty ideals. "It sounds preachy to me," he remarked, the words riding the subtle currents of skepticism, "and everything but true. I've seen your associates. Does Malachai Whitewood ring a bell?"

A contemplative pause hung between them, the weight of unspoken truths resonating within the confined space of the train car. Riven, momentarily lost in recollection, took a moment to sift through the recesses of his memories. His response, when it came, was laced with an unsettling shift in tone, as his voice involuntarily dipped into a maniacal giggle.

"It does, silly kit," he retorted, the words dripping with a disturbing playfulness. "Silly kit! Silly indeed! Small puppy. Big clothes."

The absurdity of his reply hung in the air, a disconcerting contrast to the serious undertones of their conversation.

Kieran flattened an ear, and raised a brow; all he could think of was what a nut job this man was. "Right," he remarked dryly, a disbelieving undercurrent coloring his tone.

In a decisive shift, the mint-furred fox turned toward Tessa, his touch gentle yet reassuring on her shoulder. "You're safe now," he assured her, his voice a steadfast anchor in the tumult of uncertainty that surrounded them.

The jade starlight within Tessa's eyes shimmered with a mixture of mild surprise and gratitude. A delicate smile graced her features as she acknowledged Kieran's protection. "Yea... thank you. And Kidemonas."

Kieran tilted his head. "Kidemonas?"

Tessa's grin widened, her expression animated as she shifted her gaze towards Perseus. "Mmm. When Perseus turns into his ultimate form, he abides by a second name; that's Kidemonas."

Kieran absorbed this new piece of information with a subtle nod, the intrigue in his golden eyes mirroring his curiosity. Things were coming to light, revealing the depths of the connection between Tessa and her enigmatic dragon companion. "Ah, I see," the minty fox responded, a thoughtful lilt in his voice. The revelation added a layer of mystique to their already complex journey. Turning his attention to the imposing dragon, Kieran called out in a tone that carried both respect and gratitude, "You did a good job, Kidemonas. I appreciate you helping me."

Perseus, or rather Kidemonas, acknowledged the praise with a dignified nod, one that held behind it a sense of acknowledgment, one that carried with it an understanding of honor between males.

The cavernous echoes of Kidemonas' majestic form reverberated as his mouth opened, to Kieran's surprise, the atmosphere tinged with an otherworldly energy. "You have passed the trial of loyalty, Dravenholm. I wished to see how far you'd go to protect my Astrika Propheta, that is Tessa, and you did not disappoint."

Kieran, overcome by the unexpected revelation, found himself in a speechless moment. Tessa offered a comforting rub on Kieran's arm.

"It's okay," she reassured, a gentle smile gracing her features. "I forgot to tell you that he also speaks in this form. My bad for not mentioning that."

Kieran's perceptive gaze lingered on Kidemonas, a newfound respect burgeoning within him. "So he's very intelligent then," Kieran remarked, a trace of admiration coloring his words. "Not just a combat pet."

His erratic laughter cut through the space like shards of glass, a stark contrast to the measured intelligence gleaming in Kidemonas' eyes. The flame-colored drake rose with a deliberate grace, his massive form inches from the insolent fox's face. A plume of hot steam surged forward in the form of a snort, a searing reminder of the dragon's formidable power, burning Riven lightly.

"Keep your silence, now," Kidemonas commanded, his stern tone leaving no room for dissent. The brown fox, cowed by the draconic authority, promptly closed his mouth, submitting.

Tessa's eyes held a mixture of fondness and gratitude as she shared the intricate connection she held with her celestial companion. "To answer your question, yes. Kidemonas, or Perseus, is my friend from... back home. He was assigned to me from birth by my family, and he has always protected me. He also was my study partner when my parents would have me take lessons about our race, and our country."

Kieran absorbed the intricate tapestry of revelations. His gaze shifted toward Riven, a crazed observer with a plan hidden behind his veil of lunacy. The brown fox, though seemingly unhinged, displayed a keen awareness of the dynamics at play. Bound and restrained, his deep amber eyes told of a mind that harbored schemes and stratagems, carefully concealed within the recesses of his madness.

He may be crazy but he also knew exactly what he was doing, it would appear.

"I'd suggest not talking about yourself, or Kidemonas, in front of our 'friend' over there," Kieran advised Tessa with a tone of caution, a knowing glance cast toward the enigmatic fox. Tessa, catching the subtlety in his words, complied, retreating into a quiet contemplation.

She nestled among the hay, seeking solace from the recent turmoil. She'd have the opportunity to talk more about her past when Riven wasn't present.

Turning his attention to the bound fox, Kieran approached Riven with a measured purpose. He knelt down, their eyes meeting in a silent exchange. Despite the restraint, Kieran spoke with a tone that carried both authority and a glimmer of understanding. "You have two choices now," he began, his words deliberate. "You can cooperate and answer our questions, or you can remain silent and face the consequences when we reach our destination. The latter, I assure you, won't be pleasant."

Riven's grin widened, a malevolent glint in his eyes as if the very thought of compliance amused him. "The Emberlands is an anarchist territory," he declared, the words hanging like a veiled threat.

Kieran, unfazed, met Riven's gaze with an unwavering determination. "I know," he responded evenly. "I'm not talking about the law. So, will you comply or not?"

Riven's silence stretched for a tense moment, the only sound the rhythmic clatter of the train on its tracks. Then, with an unsettling chuckle, he leaned back against the ropes that bound him, looking at Kieran with his muzzle in an upward angle.

"You've got guts, Dravenholm," Riven rasped, his tone a blend of mockery and amusement. "Alright, ask your questions. I might even answer them." His lips curled into a smile that was more a baring of teeth than any expression of mirth.

The minty fox took note of the fact that he knew his last name. Only a few from Dawnbreak know it, mainly the authorities; that in itself answered a considerable amount of questions for him.

Kieran, undeterred by Riven's theatrics, kept his gaze steady. "Who do you work for? Why is Tessa a target?"

Riven's eyes, momentarily glazed, refocused on Kieran. "Ah, now that's the question, isn't it? I'm not just a pawn, you know. As for the girl, let's just say her past is catching up with her."

Kieran's mind raced, searching for the right inquiries that might unravel the tangled web of motives. Tessa, still curled up in her corner, watched the exchange with a mixture of curiosity and lingering fear. Kieran's jaw clenched at the frustration of dealing with adversaries that insisted on being so vague.

"Enough with the nonsense. Who wants Tessa, and why?"

Riven's grin widened. "It's not just about her. It's about what she carries within her. The key to a power that can reshape worlds. As for who wants her... that is hard to explain if I were to answer you, but right now I want her."

Kieran paused. "Hmm... yes, you did say you are not a pawn. You're acting alone?" he asked.

"Correct," Riven nodded. "There isn't just one faction after your friend. Haha! Friend!" The brown fox's ear twitched rapidly, then rested.

That opened up a lot of possibilities to Kieran. It made sense; if she really did hold so much power, or was meant for such greatness, then of course everyone who knew about it would be chasing her to manipulate that power for their own ambitions or motives. "Why do you want her?" he inquired genuinely.

"That is for me to know, not you," the fox with the red bandanna stated flatly.

"Fair enough," said the bounty hunter. Riven's refusal to divulge his motives only deepened the intrigue surrounding Tessa. It was also possible that maybe this man, who had already proven himself agile and sneaky, could have found out his last name by overhearing the guards of the city, or meeting Malachai and deciding to have a go at taking Tessa himself before anyone else could. "You said the name Malachai Whitewood rang a bell. How so?"

Riven huffed. "Ugh. That bastard. He's all talk and no bite. Bite! Bite!" He cocked his head to the side in an involuntary movement.

The minty fox blinked. "You could say that. How'd you meet him?"

The cut-throat gave a half-smile. "He and I have a history, though not a good one. We used to be in a posse, grew up together. Eventually, he got himself exiled for constantly being drunk, while I stayed behind and became a high ranking member."

The name Malachai, usually spoken with a sneer, carried a weight of disdain in Riven's voice.

"Exiled for being constantly drunk, huh?" Kieran mused, a wry smile playing on his lips. "That does sound like Malachai. So, you're saying you two were once comrades, brothers even?"

Riven's eyes, a mix of derision and resentment, bore into Kieran's. "Comrades? Brothers? Maybe once. But he changed, became obsessed with power. I stood my ground, stayed true to our ideals. He was always looking for shortcuts, ways to climb the ladder faster. Dumbass got jealous of my success, and picked a fight with me one day, after being cast out."

Kieran listened intently as Riven's words painted a vivid picture of a tumultuous past. "How did that pan out for the two of you?" he asked.

"I won, of course!" Riven growled proudly, lashing his puffed up tail. "I hate that man so much. Hate him."

It was an interesting history the two shared, and he could see how it would make sense given what he'd seen of Malachai. The rapist did not seem like the most brave or capable of men, and was in actuality quite weak.

"Malachai doesn't sound like he'd be the leader of any group, so that answers some things for me. He sounds like a follower. Now, I must ask... What do you know about the corruption in Dawnbreak?" Kieran queried, liking how willing he was to talk. Compared to Whitewood, this was easy work.

Riven snorted and laughed maniacally. "You're not seriously asking me that, are you, Spearmint?" he licked his lips, and smirked. "Tellers get put in cellars. Don't you know?"

Spearmint...?' he thought, a little taken aback by the sudden nickname. He chose not to argue against it. Kieran's thoughts were a whirlwind of questions. He glanced at Tessa, who sat quietly, her starry fur shimmering in the ambient light, an enigma wrapped in uncertainty.

Riven chuckled, breaking the silence. "You're in over your head, Dravenholm. This is a game of gods, and you're just a pawn stumbling through their moves. I am not such a pawn, thankfully."

The mention of gods sent a shiver down Kieran's spine. "Fine, if you won't speak of the corruption, then enlighten me about Tessa. What power lies within her?" Kieran asked.

Riven's eyes glinted with a mixture of amusement and something darker. "The power is older than time itself. It can shape reality, rewrite destinies. Tessa is the vessel, the living key to a force that can remake the world."

Kieran did not respond, because he was at a loss for words. He failed to understand how any of this was possible. How could Tessa really hold all this world-shifting power?

"That's a load of crap and you must realize that!" Tessa exploded, with an edge of calmness to her voice. She stood up and approached, Kidemonas tensing with a sense of duty to protect. "It's just a fairy tale. These things don't exist."

Kieran raised a brow, turning toward her. "That's what I'd think, but everyone seems to think you're a goddess or something."

Riven laughed. "You know more than you let on, Astrika Propheta."

Tessa grimaced and faced away. "Lies... It's just something my parents believe in. I can't actually do anything."

Riven narrowed his amber eyes, glancing at Kidemonas and then back to her. "You can. You've been running for years, to escape your own destiny, but we all know that's impossible."

The starry fox began to shake, and her sides heaved with quickened breath, as if remembering a flood of unwelcome memories. "It is none of your concern! I'm not going with you or anyone, besides Kieran, you wild ruffian! Forget it. I belong to no one."

Riven rolled his eyes. "You're more stubborn than I had imagined, but it is no wonder you've evaded capture by the powers that be for so long, Miss Tessa."

Kieran witnessed a rage grow aflame in her jade eyes, and her fur bristled out like a bush, the starry sparkle of her fur seeming to glisten more intensely. She curled her lips. "Drop the formalities, I know you're not here to give me any respect. You were about to kill my friend, slimebag."

Tessa lashed her tail "You would have killed my dragon too, if you could have!"

"I do whatever I must," Riven argued snidely. "I have never seen you perform the powers you're rumored to possess, but mark my words, I will. I know a lot about your past, you can't talk your way out of this one. I've been hunting you for a long time."

"You'll see nothing," Tessa snarled.

"That's enough, both of you," the minty fox broke in, taking leadership in the moment. "Tessa, don't feel pressured by him, he's just a tied up rat. As for you, Brownie," he turned to the brown fox, giving him a dumb nickname just as he'd been given. "I'm not interested in much from you beyond your answers to my questions. After that, I'm tossing you off this train."

Riven looked taken aback and quite offended. "I'm sorry, what? What? Sorry!" he stumbled on his words. "I help you with what I can, and you're just going to ditch me? You, sir, are a dickhead. Dickhead! A real donkey."

"You'd be too much of a risk to keep around," Kieran explained, pointing his ears upwards. "I don't need you knowing where we're going. Besides, you're... insane."

"Ugh," Riven barked, absolutely miffed. He shifted in his uncomfortable bindings. "Judgmental!"

"I don't want you with us anyway!" Tessa raised her voice with pure attitude, amplifying her voice by speaking into her white paws at the brown fox outlaw.

"Come on, now," the outlaw subtly begged, and seemed to genuinely want to be included in their journey, "look, I'm defeated here. I've been chasing this girl for years. I really just want to see what she's capable of for myself. I've told you that I look down on Whitewood, so I must be more trustworthy than he is, right?"

"It's a possibility, but also a big risk," Kieran remarked. He had to admit that he was carefully considering letting Riven stay, he had some kind of instinct within him that it might be a good idea, but he was remaining guarded for now. It felt just as crazy as Riven was messed up in the head, but also potentially right.

'Hard decisions... hard decisions... he could be useful, having allies is important right now,' Kieran mused shortly.

"I know what you're thinking," Riven went on, flattening one ear and tilting his head slightly, furrowing a single brow. "You think something is wrong with my head, but there isn't, at least not entirely. I may have a few screws loose, but my only issue is I laugh at weird times and say strange combinations of words; if I become stressed or excited, it comes out. That is something I cannot help. Don't misjudge me."

"That is part of why I think you're crazy, but the other bit is because you went to not only kill but to bite me," Kieran stood up, towering over the brown fox, in a subconsciously dominating way. He shoved his hands into his pockets.

Riven shrugged. "Isn't that just male bonding?" he laughed, genuinely this time.

Kieran paused. Did he really think…? He audibly face-palmed. *'This guy…'* he inwardly sighed. Turning to Kidemonas, he asked, "What do you think?"

The large flame beast remained still, hot eyes locked onto Riven assertively; he appeared to think very deeply about the situation, something Kieran had not expected. He thought it more likely that Tessa's protector would immediately call for the expulsion of all danger, with how obsessively protective he was of her. A few moments passed before an answer was given by the dragon, who'd carefully considered all available options. "As much as I would revel in drenching my claws in his blood, it is also imperative to our quest, and most importantly to my Astrika Propheta's safety, that her enemies be destroyed from the face of this earth," he said solemnly, and as seriously as could be. "Gaining support from every possible source would be ideal. A network must be formed if we are to fulfill our goals. In which case, I approve of this furred nitwit; if he gives me a reason to distrust him, I won't ask permission to execute him then and there, and feast on his pearly white bones."

Riven, having been confident and brave up until that point, let slip a vibe of fear, even if for a split second before recovering and feigning like he was not afraid of the formidable beast.

"What? Are you serious?" Tessa flattened her ears, outraged. "Kidemonas!"

Kidemonas moved toward the starry fox and pulled her close to him for a snuggle. "Do not worry. You have my word, as always, that I will keep you safe."

Tessa hid her face in his white chest fluff. "He scares me..."

"Be not scared," the fire drake soothed the girl. "I will be with you at all times. He shall not hurt you; if he even thinks about it, I will erase his existence."

Kieran turned his attention from the sweet scene back over to Riven. "I think that he makes a good point, you would be useful," he stated, letting his tense muscles relax. He had not even realized they were tight until just then, to be honest.

"I'm glad you think so," Riven nodded curtly.

"If I let you out of these binds, do you promise to swear loyalty to our squad from here on out, at least until our quest is over with?" Kieran made very direct eye contact with him.

Riven took time to genuinely consider before giving his answer. "I did not think this was how today would go, but... yes, I promise. I swear it."

"Good. I will give you one chance to prove yourself," the minty fox's countenance softened and he leaned down to untie the ropes that kept the outlaw immobilized. Once he was free, Riven rubbed his arms and hand-paws, alleviating the soreness.

"Thank you," Riven reached out to shake Kieran's hand, to which the bounty hunter obliged. "Let's formally introduce ourselves, and start fresh. My name is Riven Treeglade, of the heart of Veridis, master of crimson daggers; and you?"

The mint-furred fox dipped his head in polite respect. "I'm Kieran Dravenholm, of Drakewood Heights in the Ironpeak Mountains, life-long bounty hunter. It is bittersweet to meet you."

Riven smirked cheekily. "I'll stick with Spearmint."

"Only if you want an unfortunate meeting with my daggers," Kieran twitched his whiskers, half joking. "Brownie."

Yep. It would seem they'd get along just fine. For now.

CHAPTER NINE

TALES OF ORIGINS

—★—

It seemed like the journey lasted weeks when in reality it was only a few days.

In that time, the trio got to know each other better and grew more comfortable. Kieran would not let his guard down, though; he knew that no matter how friendly someone was or how worthy of trust they seemed did not mean they actually were.

Not everything was as it seemed in many cases. Life had taught him that. For that reason, he'd remain suspicious and on high alert, just in case. Perseus, now back in his small noodle dragon form, had also seemed to make that choice, too.

In the last few days on the train, Kieran, Tessa, Perseus, and Riven had all slept in the same vicinity, ate and drank together, and told stories.

Apparently, the brown fox had been born in the Vasthaven Mesa nation, a desert territory to the south; he was a ready and able bandit, living on his own terms, doing as he pleased.

He claimed, however, that he did not steal from or kill just anyone; he took riches from those who used them for harm and killed individuals who either attacked him first or were just being a general asshole by hurting others.

Riven, through the veil of his odd behavior and his questionable motives for chasing down

Tessa, likely had a real heart of gold... or at least, to a certain degree. He had already proven to be a lot better than Malachai, and that was a welcome thing.

Kieran worried that once they reached their destination and made camp somewhere he'd turn on them all and kidnap the starry winged fox, so he'd keep an eye out.

Once they'd arrived at the train station in one of the towns of the Emberlands, one that was quite small to Kieran but was likely considered a moderately sized city to the inhabitants of this nation of mostly forested wilderness and the occasional lava flow, they exited the train car stealthily, moving quickly and keeping hidden within the crowd.

"Why would anyone come here?" Riven cringed.

"What do you mean?" Kieran asked with confusion. For him, the Emberlands were beautiful and held many memories.

Riven rotated his dark brown ears, looking ahead. "There's nothing here. It's just a small town."

Tessa chimed in. "I kind of like it here. The fewer people the better."

The minty fox decided to become a tour guide for the others momentarily. "People come here because it's a good place to do exactly that. They like to get away from it all, and just soak in the wilderness."

"Why here and not anywhere else? Other nations have plenty of wild," Riven inquired, adjusting his red bandanna and dusting off his black leather jacket.

"Because it has a lot of history. Didn't anyone ever teach you about the First Dragons and the First Foxes?" Kieran asked, honestly baffled. "The origin story of Arthos."

Riven blinked, his amber eyes showing just how confused he was; the brown fox said nothing, at a loss for what to say. The bounty hunter's mouth hung open, for he was abashed; those were important stories, ones he'd learned from his parents, many years ago.

They trudged on under the stormy sky, walking on muddy dirt roads side by side, out of the town and into the sparsely wooded hills dotted by copses outside the settlement. Their goal was to find a campsite for the night, a good place to sleep and rest their heads.

Kieran looked to Tessa, urging her with a look to join in the explanation if she felt she should, then back to Riven, and began to recount the story he'd been told. "Long ago, as the legend has it, foxes came down from the stars to find an island called Emberland. They established a colony there and had many kits to carry on their name. They loved the earth so much, but they wished it were bigger."

Riven giggled, giving way to a short outburst of loud laughter. "Yea! We all do."

Kieran continued, taking the lead in front of both of them but always looking over his shoulder, while also scanning the land for a potential spot to settle down. "One day, dragons arrived from the stars too; they wanted Emberland for themselves, and the star foxes fought them. The dragons destroyed the island, covering it in fire, and making volcanoes erupt, sending lava flows into homes."

Tessa grew rigid at the mention of the star foxes, and Kieran noticed it; he wondered why but he would have to ask later, away from Riven's ears. "Then, when all hope seemed to be lost, one fox named Asprochioni rose to the plate, touched by the spirits of snow and the spirits of stars. He moved the earth around him, closing up the volcanoes, and causing lush forests to grow atop the lava beds. The dragons he brought to the ground and used large rocks to tie them down. He sealed their mouth with starchain, a starry substance not of this world that works like a chain but is unbreakable unless the creator of it dies.”

Riven scowled. “Ugh, this sounds like a dumb nursery rhyme or something my mother would tell me. Do you really believe any of this?”

“Well,” Kieran thought for a moment and paused, then answered. “I am not sure. I just know that this is what everyone is told, and it is why people come here; to see the place that started it all. There’s a monument in the main town back there, to honor Asprochioni.”

“It’s stupid,” Riven laughed. “Foxes? From the sky? Come on.”

Tessa pouted.

Riven noticed, and Kieran watched. “What’s the matter, missy? You don’t believe the stories of your ancestors now, do you?” the outlaw asked, seeming to be hinting at a greater point than he let on. He'd come here seeking Tessa for her powers, that much was clear, so he had to believe in its existence, right? Or, was he here for something else, like gaining status simply because many chose to believe in her powers?

'Wait, no... Riven told Tessa that he would see her perform her alleged powers and that he knew a lot about her past,' the bounty hunter contemplated the complexity of this interaction. *'Something's gotta be going on... it doesn't add up.'*

"N-no, of course not!" the winged fox lashed out defensively.

Thunder rumbled softly above in the gray, sodden clouds.

"Good," Riven laughed, holding his head high, raindrops beginning to drip down through the rivulets of his facial scars. "Only a weak idiot would believe in children's fairy tales."

Tessa's brows remained furrowed down. It was clear that the brown fox's words struck a nerve with her, but Kieran could not pinpoint exactly why. It was obvious she was sensitive about her past, that much had already been made known to him, but he was missing a lot of key details... ones that Tessa preferred to keep under lock and key within her heart.

She was running, after all, and maybe not entirely just from power-hungry figures.

The camp had been set up in a small ravine, within a large hollow log; it acted as a worthy shelter from the unending rain, a place of

warmth, and it smelled quite nicely of pine within its natural walls.

There was plenty of room for everyone to lay down comfortably. Kieran and Tessa slept that night with their blankets, but Riven, having nothing with him, made his bed on the bare inner bark. He did not seem to mind it, though; he was quite a hardened individual, and highly adaptable.

He had boasted that he'd slept on much worse.

Perseus rested huddled very close to Tessa, though in all actuality probably never actually fell into slumber; he had the same concerns as Kieran in that he feared the new addition of their squad would kidnap his friend, the one he was sworn to protect.

The dragon kept guard with his loyalty and his love.

Kieran, for some reason, had not been able to stay asleep and so he sat up for a moment, to spend time thinking until he felt ready to try again. An extra set of eyes and ears to keep guard was always a good thing, anyway.

He noticed that Riven's scent became fainter and fainter as the next hour passed, and when the realization hit him that the newcomer was no longer nearby him or within the tree shelter he tensed up and felt a fear that coursed through his entire body like electricity.

The minty fox quickly looked around in the very dim lighting to see if Tessa and her dragon were still with him, and she was. Some light bounced onto his form, just barely, and if he listened carefully he could hear her breathing.

This relieved him and calmed his heart, but the question still nagged at him like briars against his back in the wind; where had Riven gone?

'Maybe for a piss in the middle of the night,' Kieran huffed humorously, deciding to wait around ten minutes for his return. It was pouring hard, so surely if he just needed to relieve himself he'd be back by now.

No fox would want to stay out in weather like this.

When Riven did not return, the question burned stronger in Kieran's mind. Had he abandoned them? Had he gone to the local town? Worse yet, did he know anyone in these parts, was there anyone waiting here, who would help him take Tessa? His mind swirled with the possibilities.

To be safe, Kieran whispered to the fire drake. "I'm going outside to look for Riven. Signal for me with a roar if I am needed."

He removed his clothing so that only his minty fur was exposed, so that when he went outside in the rain he wouldn't get his attire wet.

The soil was wet and soggy as the minty fox pressed his paw pads into it with every step. His ears were attuned to the sounds around him, and his golden eyes were sharp on the lookout for any visual changes.

He tried to follow Riven's scent but the rain had bogged it down and diluted it greatly. Still, he pursued. Kieran was good at this. The determination paid off and he found paw tracks leading up a muddy path on a hill with scattered rocks adorning the ground in patches.

Following it, he picked up the faintest indications of Riven through scent; he was getting closer.

The mud splashed with a consistency almost like water due to the amount of heavy rain the region was getting.

A fresh, earthy scent caressed Kieran's nostrils, the smell of raindrops against green pine needles and grayish-brown mossy tree bark. This place reminded Kieran of his home in Drakewood Heights, except it was just missing all the snow.

The terrain twisted and turned, curved up and down, and Kieran had to bob between the foliage. Pine needles and cones mottled the forest floor, and crisp crunches were heard as Kieran moved forward, even in the rain.

Ahead of the bounty hunter was a meadow, with a shadowed figure standing completely still before another figure that he couldn't quite identify. *'Riven?'* he thought, trying to make out the fox's features in the dark of the stormy night.

A flash of lightning streamed overhead behind the clouds, illuminating the figure in the meadow for just a moment, long enough for Kieran to get a good look at him. The detail that stuck out most was brown fur; the unclothed body of Riven.

Riven was standing in front of what seemed to be a statue, just staring at it.

The bounty hunter had, of course, not gone weaponless; he still wore his belt of leather, with the sheaths for his daggers attached. Kieran approached the outlaw with caution, hand paws resting upon the hilts of his blades, ready to draw them at a moment's notice if he had to.

"I was wondering where you were," Kieran called out to him, walking out of the undergrowth.

Riven bristled at the voice of the bounty hunter, but quickly calmed when he saw that it was only the leader of the group. "Yo."

Kieran got close enough to see that the statue was of a female fox draped in luxurious clothing, holding up a big star in one hand and a moon in the other. Indications of snow were carved at her feet paws, and the statue as a whole was made of iron. The minty fox couldn't help but notice that her breasts were barely covered by the draped material. In the place of her eyes were jade gemstones.

Engraved at the lower half of the statue, below the girl, was:

TO THE MOTHER OF OUR PEOPLE
ASTRIKA PROPHETA

Kieran lit up and perked up his ears. "That's the name Kidemonas said on the train!" he exclaimed, shifting his gaze to the outlaw beside him.

"Indeed, indeed," Riven said, not making eye contact with Kieran, then creased his lips in a smile. "I wonder; if Tessa saw this, would she finally believe in her destiny, or would she keep running away from it?"

"Wait, you believe in all that?" Kieran asked, apprehensive and surprised.

"Of course," Riven answered. "Earlier it was just a show."

"Why?"

A chill wind blew against their bodies, the red wildflowers in the meadow dancing to and fro.

"She needs folk to do that," he reasoned.

"Tessa has been running for a long time, and she believes in everything her family taught her, but she's scared."

Kieran wanted to ask so many different questions such as how Riven knew all of this, but held his tongue. "What could she be scared of?" he asked.

Riven's eyes widened for a moment and he took in a deep breath, then laughed. "Imagine you have to commune with the God Iesu and go to war with literal demons to save your home," he explained. "That's what Tessa had to grow up with, knowing full well that she could lose her life in the process. It was likely terrifying for her, and a hard load to bear."

"I did not know that," Kieran commented in a low voice. "So, then, if you believe in all this, why did you come after her?"

Riven glared the minty-furred fox dead in the face, serious as could be, the scars covering his body evident in the angle and lighting. "Let me make this clear; I won't say it again," he grumbled. "I have known about her for many years and wished she'd chosen a different path for the sake of all. When I saw her with you at the train station, I hopped aboard because I did not want her with another ambitious fox. I waited for the right moment, then struck so that I could take her for myself, to keep her safe and maybe change her mind. Then when her drake attacked me, I knew that I had been mistaken; you are her savior, not I."

Kieran took a deep breath. "A pleasant thing to hear, though not something I had expected."

The level of trust that the bounty hunter had in the outlaw was ever-so-slowly growing, and gaining traction.

There was always the possibility that he was telling a very elaborate lie, but based on his tone and mannerisms, as well as how this answered his question from earlier on the road, he chose to put some faith in it.

He would not fully trust Riven until their relationship had been well-weathered, and that would take time, but this was a fine starting point.

"That is fine," Riven began to trail his fingers along the jade stones of the Astrika Propheta.

Kieran watched in silence.

The brown fox looked back at him. "What about you?" he asked.

"Excuse me?"

"Why do you have her if you're not one of the shady ones?"

Kieran answered quickly. "She's with me because it's part of my job. I'm a bounty hunter, and right now my job is to keep her away from the corrupt men in Dawnbreak."

Riven grinned mischievously, lashing his tail. "Ah, yes! However, there's a hole in your story."

Kieran flattened his ears.

"You don't believe in Tessa's powers, do you? You're an atheist."

"I never said that."

"By your very nature, you deny everything she is," the outlaw challenged him. "If you thought it was just a rumor, then why not let her succumb to the forces that be? Their expectations of her would be shot dead like a sick horse, and they'd simply find another use for her or kill her then and there for knowing too much about their little cult. Cult! Cult activity!"

Kieran narrowed his golden eyes, remaining still. "What are you getting at?"

Riven laughed crazily, his signature at this point. Kieran had begun to get used to it. "Dravenholm, you've either begun to believe in the Lord above," he said, pointing upward to the sky, "or you care for the girl."

"I do care for her, she's an innocent bystander, and I rescued her from a weaved web of power struggles," he responded, not hesitating one bit.

Riven rolled his eyes and snorted. "Not that kind of care, ya' northerner. I mean the kind you feel in your pants."

"No."

"You risked your life for her."

"I risked it for my job."

Riven sighed heavily and turned away. "Alright. Then you're the first man I've ever met who's gotten a hard-on for his job. Congratulations."

Kieran grumbled in annoyance and protested. "It's not like that. I could care less about her, I-"

"You don't need to explain it to me," the brown-furred fox stated with a light-hearted tone. "I received all the answers I needed. Have you received all of yours?"

"I could say I'm satisfied," the minty fox dipped his head curtly. "For now."

Riven cracked a smile and walked on past the bounty hunter, toward the forest they'd come out from. "I'm tired. You coming?"

He watched the outlaw for a moment, thunder roaring above.

Riven wasn't half-bad, but he sure was aggravating; a strong comrade, no doubt useful in the future to his quest.

Hopefully, all Kieran had to deal with going forward was the outlaw's blaring tomfoolery. "Yeah," the conflicted bounty hunter responded, trotting ahead to catch up. "Let's get back to camp."

KEEP A
LOOK OUT
FOR BOOK 2

CHAPTER ONE

TALES OF ORIGINS

Dawn painted the Emberlands in hues of amber and gold as the squad trudged through the damp terrain. The scent of pine lingered in the air, blending with the earthy aroma of wet soil. The tranquility, however, was shattered by a haunting howl that echoed through the hills, through the tree branches in the copses.

Kieran's ears perked up, and he instinctively reached for the hilt of the two daggers strapped to his sides. The squad came to a sudden halt, eyes scanning the surroundings. In the early light, shadows danced among the trees, and the distant howls grew louder, closer.

"They're closing in," Kieran whispered to his companions, the urgency in his voice cutting through the crisp morning air. "We're surrounded. Ready your weapons!"

He withdrew the bow from his back, arrows at the ready.

Riven, with his two ruby daggers gleaming in the cool light, nodded in acknowledgment. "Let them come. We'll show them what happens when they mess with us."

The first wolves emerged from the trees, their fur mottled with shades of gray and brown. Hungry eyes fixated on the four, and wild growls rumbled through the pack.

Kieran's minty fur bristled as he crouched, his golden gaze locked onto the approaching predators. One wolf, larger than the others, led the hunt, one with dark fur and green eyes.

"Stay close," he commanded, his eyes darting between Riven, Tessa, and Perseus. Tessa clutched her dagger tightly, her wings twitching with nervous energy. Perseus, ready to transform at a moment's notice, crouched protectively beside her.

The wolves lunged at them from all sides, jaws agape and claws unfurled. Kieran, with the grace of a seasoned hunter, dodged the snapping jaws of the first assailant.

Before it could attack again, he took aim and shot it through its skull, between the eyes. He returned the bow onto his back again, and retrieved his daggers. His trusty blades danced in his hands, swift and lethal.

Riven, a whirlwind of motion, swift as a hummingbird and as deadly as a cobra, met the pack head-on, his ruby daggers slicing through fur and sinew.

Tessa, her movements surprisingly agile, ducked and dodged, her dagger finding its mark with precision.

Perseus, sensing the imminent danger, transformed into Kidemonas, a magnificent fire drake larger than a horse.

Fire met fur as Kidemonas unleashed a torrent of flames, fending off the encroaching wolves. The scent of singed pelt filled the air, and the predators recoiled in a disarray of high-pitched whines, momentarily disoriented.

Blood drizzled down Kieran's hand paws, the stench of iron in the dewy air. This moment weaved a web of hardship for him and everyone with him, and would no doubt bring them all closer. The squad stood at a defensive position, ready to strike and kill their enemies, back against back and facing all directions.

The alpha wolf eyed Kieran, sensing his dominance over the others. Leader against leader, he prowled to and fro, snarling and drooling from his crimson-stained maw, looking for a weak spot in the minty-furred fox.

Kieran readied himself. The alpha leapt straight at him, and was met with a knife wound to the shoulder. The wolf did not care, he bit onto Kieran's neck, causing him immense pain and drawing blood, shaking him violently.

MEET THE AUTHOR

Hello! My name is Achak, but I sometimes go by Kovateisus. I write fantasy and adventure stories, do graphic novels/comics, as well as Christian non-fiction. I am 25 years old, married, live in New Hampshire, and have a lovely West German working-line King Shepherd named Selah. I really love theropod dinosaurs, as well as wolves and foxes.